Mail C

Christian Mail Order Brides Collection

MONTANA WEST

Published by Global Grafx Press, LLC. © 2015

All Biblical quotations used in this manuscript are taken from the King James Bible or the English Standard Version of the Bible.

No part of this publication may be reproduced in any form or by any electronic or mechanical means, including scanning, photocopying, or otherwise without prior written permission of the copyright holder, except by a reviewer who may quote brief passages in a review.

Copyright © 2015 by Montana West

All Rights Reserved.

ISBN-10: 1507782926
ISBN-13: 978-1507782927

CONTENTS

CHAPTER ONE
CHAPTER TWO
CHAPTER THREE
CHAPTER FOUR
CHAPTER FIVE
CHAPTER SIX
CHAPTER SEVEN
CHAPTER EIGHT
CHAPTER NINE
CHAPTER TEN
CHAPTER ELEVEN
A MAIL ORDER MARRIAGE MISTAKE
ABOUT THE AUTHOR

CHAPTER ONE

BOSTON, MASSACHUSSETTS
END OF WINTER, 1874

Elizabeth wished someone would wake her up from this horrible dream. Her world had come crashing down around her, and she did not know what to do or how to face the future. Though grief washed through her, clouding her chubby, round face, she could not bring herself to cry. Her father was dead, and now Gerald Hawkins, his attorney for longer than Elizabeth had been alive, sat across from her in his lavish office, rubbing his palms on the thighs of his trousers with an expression that boded more bad news.

Elizabeth Lowell was nineteen years old, but anyone looking at her at the moment would have thought she was a decade older: her face was so lined with age, pain and anxiety. She perched on the edge of the seat and blinked owlishly from behind her large glasses.

Gerald said, "Miss Lowell. Miss Elizabeth. I am so sorry for your loss."

"Is that why you called me here? You conveyed your condolences at the funeral."

"Yes. I did."

Gerald had been Elizabeth's father Benjamin's attorney for over thirty years, and having to give the deceased man's daughter more bad news saddened him deeply. Benjamin had been a very astute and wealthy businessman, with a knack for smelling new opportunities and grabbing at them. In a short span of time, the man had become very rich. But all that had changed when his wife died ten years ago. It was as though the light had been snuffed out of him. He had lost his touch and died with only debts to his name. Not that his two daughters knew the latter. Not yet.

"Is this about who will be running my father's factory? Because I cannot be of much service in that. Surely my father notated such things in his will?"

"He did."

Elizabeth stared at him. A light sheen of sweat shone on her forehead, and she pulled a handkerchief from her bag, twisting it between her hands. "Mr. Hawkins. You'd best tell me."

"If your father's death hadn't been so sudden, I'm certain he would have done more to mitigate things. To prepare you." Mr. Lowell took a deep breath. "As it is, I've done everything I can in order to give you and your sister time for your grief."

"It's only been two weeks."

"But you will have to vacate your home, and there will be an auction for your father's things—"

"What are you saying?"

"Your father died a pauper, Elizabeth. You and your sister…he left nothing."

"Nothing—" Elizabeth took a sharp breath. "Nothing! But what are we to do?"

The elderly man shook his head sadly. "I am sorry that in the last ten years your father made unwise business decisions and choices, and he got himself into very deep debt. I advised him to sell off a number of the assets that he had in order to settle some of the debts, and in that way he could have been able to at least have something left over to start again but," Gerald twisted his lips, "you know just how stubborn your father could be."

Elizabeth nodded. She knew her father too well. "Then what will happen to us?"

"Do you perhaps have relatives who might take you in, at least for a short while?" But even as Gerald asked, he knew this was a futile suggestion. In all the years that he had been Benjamin Lowell's attorney, the man had not mentioned any relatives from his side or his wife's side. His will had bequeathed everything to his two daughters, a will that, right now, was not even worth the paper it was written on.

"Papa was an only child, and Mama," Elizabeth sighed. She shook her head sadly. "Mama as you know was from England, and when she and Papa got married her English family disowned her, for at the time she was betrothed to a lord, or something like that. Her family never forgave her for slighting them by marrying a commoner."

"I am sorry, Miss Elizabeth." Gerald truly was sorry, especially in the light of the other news that he was about to relay to the young woman.

"Maybe if we earn enough from the sale of his possessions, we can perhaps keep the house? Rent out some rooms so that we can have an income, and then Virginia and I can stay in the servant's section because, of course, we have decided to let the servants go. There is not much work to be done now that Papa is gone. No more entertaining and all." She nodded, forcing a smile. "We can run a boarding house," she said with some hope, but this was soon dashed when she looked at the lawyer's face.

"The house must be sold. It is the only asset that your father had not mortgaged and the bank is demanding a very hefty sum, and all the other assets that he owned will not cover it. That, together with paying off the servants, will leave you and your sister with a little less than fifty dollars."

"What?"

"I am sorry child, more sorry than you will ever know. Mrs. Hawkins and I can take you in for a while, until you are grounded again," he offered, but Elizabeth shook her head.

"We will manage. Somehow." Elizabeth stood up and drew her shawl closer, the cold chilling her very bones. It was more than the cold that chilled her. It was a heart that was filled with so much dread and despair that she shuddered.

"Miss Elizabeth, the bank's representative will be by the house later today to do an inventory of all the items in the house. And you will have to leave the house after that, because I will be handing the keys over to him."

Elizabeth sat down again. "Are we to lose everything then?"

"I am sorry, child." Gerald took out his handkerchief from his coat pocket and wiped his face. It was a chilly day but he was sweating. "I wish there was something I could do, but this is beyond my control."

Elizabeth stepped into the cold Boston streets. Her five-foot, three-inch frame stooped so much beneath the weight of her grief and this terrible news that she looked like an old woman. It was drizzling, but she did not feel it as started for home. The house! It was not her house anymore. And worse, she had to tell her sister the news. Elizabeth had not wanted Virginia to accompany her to the attorney's office because her sister was more interested in her personal appearance than business. And now Elizabeth was glad her sister had not come. Virginia had a flair for the dramatic, and in her emotional state right now the last thing Elizabeth would have wanted was to cope with her swooning sister.

The sounds that usually cheered Elizabeth now sounded like death knells to her young ears. The cries of the newspaper boys made Elizabeth hurry. Obviously the state of her father's misfortunes would be splashed all over the papers and she needed to get away from the house and hide before the neighbors and other acquaintances showed up with their pitying faces.

Another reason for her hurry was so that she could get some things out of the house before the bank representative swooped in and grabbed everything.

When Elizabeth got home she stopped for a moment outside the gate and looked at what had been her home for all her life. She seemed oblivious to the fact that she was now drenched, and the water ran in rivulets down the sides of her head, making her hair even more curly than it usually was. She had been born in this house, as had her sister. She had thought it was a happy house, but now it looked like a doomed house. Her mother had died in this house, her father had died in this house, and now everything they owned was being taken away, leaving them with nothing.

"It must be a cursed house," she thought as she opened the gate slowly and walked up the short pathway, and climbed the three steps wearily. She sat for a moment on the porch seat and looked around, noticing the wilting flowers in the garden that had been her mother's joy and pride and which Elizabeth had tended to lovingly in memory of her dear mother. Since her father's death she had not been near the garden and now never would be.

"Oh, Mama," she whispered, then blinked rapidly so that she would not cry. It would not do to cry at this moment. She still had to tell Virginia the dreadful news.

And true to form Virginia swooned, and Elizabeth rushed to her room to get some smelling salts which soon revived the fifteen-year-old girl.

"What are we going to do? We are ruined and will be the laughing stock of all Boston. Oh, I cannot bear it, I cannot bear this," her normally strong voice rose shrilly, and Elizabeth longed to slap her face.

"Pull yourself together. I suggest that you go to you room and grab everything that you want to take out of this house before those vultures come and take everything away." Elizabeth walked to the door. "Mr. Hawkins told me the bank representative will be coming this afternoon, and we have to leave the house immediately after the inventory is done. No doubt they do not want us to 'steal' anything that now belongs to them."

"I won't leave. Where will we go? What will we do?"

"Virginia, if you do not get off that couch and do as I have told you, I will come over there and slap you silly."

"You are just mean," Virginia started crying, and Elizabeth sighed. She walked back and sat down next to her sister.

"I am sorry, Ginnie. I wish all this was not happening. But it has happened, and we have to make the most of things, and salvage whatever is left of our lives. We will be alright, you will see." She pulled her sister close and hugged her. Virginia clutched on to her sister as though she was her lifeline. She was terrified.

"We will be alright, little girl," Elizabeth murmured soothingly. "You will see."

But later that afternoon when Mr. Hawkins and the bank's representative, who had introduced himself as Richard Slip, had gone through every one of the rooms in the house and locked each door after doing the inventory, Elizabeth felt her strength waning. It had humiliated her to walk through the house that she had loved, pointing out all the items that were in each room. She remembered all the parties they had held when her mother was alive, which had become fewer after her death. The holidays and celebrations and her coming-out party, which had been the talk of the town for many days.

Elizabeth was more uncomfortable at the leering way in which

Mr. Slip was looking at her. His beady eyes had seemed to undress her, never mind that she was very decently dressed and had a thick shawl around her shoulders. Once or twice, when Mr. Hawkins had not been looking, he had patted her bottom and she had hissed in disgust, and thereafter made it a point to walk as far away from him as she possibly could.

Virginia was seated on the porch, refusing to enter the house. She wept silently, clutching her small purse, in which was a paper that she held onto dearly. She had not even picked one dress or pair of shoes from her bedroom, forcing Elizabeth to hurriedly pack both of their clothes into her *portmanteau* which she had then dragged out of the house, and which was now lying in a rooming house just down the street from their house. From time to time the younger girl slipped her hand into the purse and took the paper out and looked at it, bringing on a fresh outpouring of tears.

It was the program for her coming-out dinner, scheduled to be held in two weeks' time but which had been cancelled when her father died. She had been looking forward to being presented and hopefully would have found herself a suitable husband. Now that would never happen. No one in their circles would want to be associated with them now that they were poor and being turned out of their house.

"Is that all there is to see?" Mr. Slip asked when the trio once again assembled in the sitting room.

"Yes, sir," Elizabeth said quietly, wishing this would all end and she could leave the presence of this man who made her skin crawl.

"And the servants' quarters? Is there nothing of value there?"

"I am afraid not, sir," she shook her head.

"I want to see the rooms anyway."

Elizabeth looked at Mr. Hawkins who nodded silently, and she led the way out of the sitting room and into the corridor to the kitchen. Mr. Slip looked around and noted all the items in the kitchen, checked all the cabinets and wrote down in the notebook he carried, and then motioned for her to lead the way once again. As Elizabeth had said there was nothing of much value in the four servants' rooms, save for the metal beds and cabinets in each room.

When the house was secured and the keys handed over to Mr. Slip, Mr. Hawkins took his leave because he had to go home.

Mr. Slip smiled lecherously at Elizabeth. "What a fine young woman you are!" He reached out a hand and pinched her cheek, and she hissed at him.

"You have what you need, leave me alone."

"I could make you a very happy, girl." He licked his lips, and reminded Elizabeth of a fat, ugly toad, and she almost giggled. "I can put you and your sister up in very fine quarters, and take good care of you always."

"I would rather starve on the streets of Boston than be wed to a toad like you."

Richard laughed loudly. "Who said anything about marriage? No, woman. I want you to be my mistress."

"In your nightmares," she hissed and walked to her sister. "Virginia, let us go."

"I don't want to go," Virginia whined, and Elizabeth felt all the patience run out of her.

"Get up this instant," she barked and Virginia, who had never heard that tone in her sister's voice, scrambled to her feet. Elizabeth pushed her down the steps.

"If you change your mind, which I know you soon will, seeing as you have never done an honest day's work in your life, you know where to find me."

Elizabeth's response was to grab her sister's hand and quickly walk away, trying to block out the man's mocking laughter which followed her down the street.

~~~ *** ~~~

Elizabeth ran her hands lovingly over her violin. Her father had bought it for her when she turned seven, two years before her mother had died, and Regina Lowell, who had been a good violinist, had taught her daughter the basics of playing the instrument. After she died Benjamin had paid for an Italian immigrant to teach Elizabeth, and by the time the girl was thirteen she could play the violin very well. Whenever they had guests she entertained them, and everyone agreed that she would be a professional violinist one day.

Elizabeth had wanted to play in an orchestra from the time her father had taken her and Virginia to see 'Swans on the Lake,' a production by the Boston Orchestra. This was on her fourteenth birthday and she had dedicated her time to practicing seriously, dreaming of the day when she would walk on to a stage and be given a standing ovation for her expertise.

Now all of that was a distant dream. This violin, and her mother's Bible and prayer book, were the only items that she had thought valuable enough to take from the house, apart from some clothes. This was her papa's gift to her, and it was made by a skilled craftsman and could have fetched a tidy sum of money, but she would never part with it. And she had taken it out of the house because no one had a right to it. It was hers, her property.

She wished she could play and soothe her hurting heart but the rooming house had strict rules. No children, no animals, no instruments, no noise.

"It feels like a prison," Virginia had said and broken down once again.

Indeed it felt like a prison, but Elizabeth was glad they had a roof over their heads. As much as Mrs. Little was strict, she was also very kind and looked after the girls. In the one week that they had been here she had ensured that the male boarders did not bother them at all. And she provided breakfast and dinner for the two girls and did not charge them anything extra. Elizabeth thanked her over and over again, but Mrs. Little always brushed her gratitude aside.

"It is the Christian thing to do, seeing as you have no home," she would respond. But unknown to the two girls, Mr. Hawkins had promised to pay her a dollar each week to ensure that the girls had food and that they were well taken care of.

The fifty dollars that Mr. Hawkins had given them after the sale of their house was slowly dwindling as Virginia demanded for things and Elizabeth, filled with compassion for her sister, did not want her crying so much. She catered to her sister's every whim.

The young lady stood up and put her violin back in its case. "One day soon," she kissed the tips of her fingers and touched her violin. "One day, you and I will go places and be happy again." She adjusted her glasses.

She was going to see Mr. Hawkins because he had promised to find her some work to do. He had suggested that she use her education to help transcribe letters and other important documents for people who could neither read nor write, and had told her that he would get her customers.

"Come in, Miss Elizabeth." Gerald smiled fondly at the young lady. "Mrs. Hawkins sends you her love and says that you and Virginia should come to the house for tea on Sunday, after church."

"Thank you Mr. Hawkins, we will be glad to come."

"I got some work for you to do."

"Oh, thank you so much, sir," Elizabeth beamed. "When can I begin?"

"Right away," Gerald said as he stood up. "Mrs. Summer is an elderly lady whose husband died a few weeks ago, and her only son went to the west in search of gold. She wants to send him a message to return home, but she cannot write. I told her that you would do the work for her for twenty-five cents."

"Thank you so much, sir."

Elizabeth soon settled into her work and she was glad that she at least had some money coming in because it kept her and Virginia off the streets. But after two weeks she realized that the money was not going to be enough to cater to their needs, especially now that spring was coming. They had left the house with winter clothing which would be unsuitable for spring, not to mention summer. She had managed to get only one suitcase full of clothes for them. Their father had bought them expensive gowns, and Elizabeth knew those would be sold off to settle some of the debts. Most of them had been almost new, because each time Mr. Lowell had entertained he bought his daughters new clothes.

She counted out her money as she sat on the bed in their room. She had written eight letters and now had two dollars. She reached for the purse that she hid under the mattress and when she opened it she frowned. She was sure she had left ten dollars in there that morning but now there were only five dollars left.

"Virginia," she thought. "What does she need the money for?"

Elizabeth shook her head. Her sister was proving to be quite complex, but Elizabeth soon quashed the thoughts. Virginia was a child whose world had been cruelly turned upside down and it would take her a while to adjust.

She put the two dollars with the other five, intending to give the money to Mrs. Little later when she went down for dinner. Their rent was due. The room was one dollar per day and Mrs. Little had said Elizabeth could pay her every Friday. There would be nothing left over until she got the next job, but she was determined that they would always have a roof over their heads. She had promised her mother that she would always look after Virginia.

Elizabeth sighed when she thought about her sister. Virginia was a very beautiful girl, but sometimes Elizabeth thought she was vain and spoiled. She got her looks from their mother who had been a beauty in her days. Standing at five-feet, nine-inches, the girl carried herself regally and always said she would be a famous singer one day, with a rich husband to support her. She had inherited their mother's green eyes and honey blond hair which she liked to brush and leave flowing around her shoulders. Elizabeth took after their father who had been short and stocky, with unruly, curly blond hair, thanks to his Irish ancestry.

Elizabeth was determined to support Virginia and give her all she needed, but try as much as she did the money that she got from transcribing was very little, and it was with a downcast face that she approached Mrs. Little in the third week of their arrival.

"Mrs. Little, I am sorry that I cannot give you our rent this week. Work is so hard to find."

Mrs. Little tightened her lips. "Why not take on another job, if that one that you go to everyday is not paying you?"

"I have tried, Mrs. Little. I went to the schools to offer my services to tutor the children, but they want people who are more qualified, and besides, they also want references, and I have none."

"Oh, child," Mrs. Little sighed. "I can offer you a job here, and in turn you and your sister can stay here rent-free."

"What kind of work, Mrs. Little?"

"My scullery maid, idiot that she is, ran off to get married to some miner in the west, and now I do not have anyone to wash the pots and pans, and clean the kitchen. I am willing to pay you five dollars a week, and you get your room free and you also get breakfast and dinner for the two of you."

"How can I thank you, Mrs. Little?"

"Hush, child. What I suggest is that every morning you go to your other job, and then by three o'clock you come back here to clean the morning dishes and prepare for dinner, and then wash the dinner dishes as well." The woman sighed. "But you will have to move out of the room you are staying in so that I can rent it out, and you can use Chloe's old room. It has one bed, which is large enough for the two of you to share."

By the time Elizabeth got to bed each day she was so exhausted that she stopped only long enough to take off her apron and frock, and fall into bed. She always found Virginia asleep and was glad that the young girl was getting good rest and looking happier.

But two weeks later Elizabeth was not smiling when she realized what was making Virginia happy. One night she woke up to find that she was alone in the bed, and thinking that Virginia must have gone to the outhouse, she turned over to sleep once again. However, she got up at around four o'clock when she heard the door opening, and was in time to see Virginia creeping into the room, still fully clothed.

"What are you doing up at this time?" Elizabeth struggled to sit up in bed and Virginia gave a start, dropping her purse. Elizabeth lit the candle that was beside the bed.

"You frightened me," the young girl tried to say with a laugh. "I have a running stomach."

"Really? Why did you get dressed then?"

"I did not want to go out in my petticoats, so I threw this dress over them." Elizabeth looked at her sister in the lightening room and sighed.

Something troubled Elizabeth at the way her sister seemed to have changed. Elizabeth went through her sister's things and realized that Virginia had acquired some very expensive clothes, nothing that the little money she usually took from Elizabeth's purse could pay for.

"What is this girl up to?" she wondered as she scrubbed the pots that evening. "I must find out where Virginia is getting these expensive things." Dread filled her heart when she imagined that Virginia might have met a rich old man who was giving her all these gifts in return for her body.

When she asked her sister about the expensive items, the

younger girl told her some kind ladies at the church had given her the clothes and shoes, and for a while Elizabeth believed her. But when she found face powder and lipstick among the things, she realized Virginia was lying to her. None of the ladies in church used such items. Something else was going on.

"I will kill that girl," Elizabeth fumed, but decided that she would not ask her because Virginia would just lie to her. Instead she decided that she would watch her and see, and her patience was soon rewarded.

One Saturday, Virginia got out of bed, thinking that Elizabeth was asleep. She dressed in the darkness and silently opened the door and snuck out. But this time Elizabeth was waiting for her, and gave her a few minutes head start before she threw on a thick coat and crept out after her.

Virginia, oblivious to the fact that she had a shadow, walked briskly down the dark street and slipped into an alley, with Elizabeth following her at a discreet distance. When Elizabeth got to the alley, she peered into the poorly lit street, not seeing her sister, and she got very worried. Was her sister visiting a brothel? Then she saw it. The sign said 'Wild West Tavern' and Elizabeth wondered if that was where her sister had gone. She hid in the shadows and drew closer, and soon heard a familiar voice singing.

She could not believe that Virginia was singing in the seedy tavern, and she slipped in, praying that no one would notice her.

And sure enough, there was her sister, dressed in a very tight fitting gown, her face heavily made-up, and she was dancing seductively on the stage, as men whistled and one or two joined her on the stage, pawing her, and far from being offended, the young girl giggled.

Elizabeth wanted to march to the stage and grab her sister, but she realized that the kind of crowd that was in the tavern was not the kind that would take kindly to such an interruption, and so she slipped out of the tavern and went to the rooming house, where she spent the rest of the night on her knees, sobbing her heart out in prayer.

"Oh Lord," she wept over and over again. "Do not forsake me in my hour of need. You are our Father, we have no one else. What do I do about Virginia? Lord, I do not want my sister to go down a dark path, and end up as a ruined and fallen woman. But what do I do? How can I stop her from going to that place? Please help me," she sobbed.

By the time Virginia crept into the room early in the morning Elizabeth was calm, and resolved not to let the younger girl know that she had discovered her secret. She knew that in Virginia's present state of mind the girl might even take it into her head to run away. So Elizabeth continued as if nothing was wrong, but she spent sleepless nights on her knees praying for her sister, with the result that she soon had bags under her eyes for lack of sleep.

Meanwhile, Virginia went on as before, unaware that her actions were causing her sister so much distress. But not for long. She got a very bad cold and could not sing or rise from the bed, and Elizabeth silently gave thanks for this malady that had put her sister down.

The doctor came and pronounced that Virginia had an inflammation of the lungs. "This weather is not good for your sister. You need to get her to a warmer place, if you can."

"Thank you, doctor," Elizabeth said with a sad smile. Where was she to take Virginia? Virginia had always been a sickly child, and this was especially aggravated by spring.

As Elizabeth nursed Virginia back to health, an idea began forming in her mind. While working in the kitchen scrubbing pots and pans, she had become friends with Matilda, who was the cook.

"A fine lass like you should not be scrubbing too much in someone else's kitchen. If you could only go west, you might find yourself a mighty dandy farmer to wed you, and you can then scrub in your own home. 'Tis a great shame," she 'tsked' over and over again.

At first Elizabeth had laughed and ignored her, but then as she watched her sister tossing and turning in bed she decided that she would ask Matilda for more details. Matilda was only too pleased to pass on more information.

"Chloe, the one that was here before you, got herself a man from the west, and left."

"How?"

"The newspapers. Men in the west are always putting 'adverts' in the papers to find mail-order brides. I reckon if you get hold of the Boston Daily, you might find yourself a man, my dear lass."

And the very next day Elizabeth took some of her savings and bought a newspaper. But the adverts that were there for mail-order brides did not appeal to her. The men seemed to only want women to clean, cook and breed. Besides, none of the men professed to be Christians, and the last thing Elizabeth wanted was to be wed to a pagan. The cleaning and cooking part was not bad. It was the breeding part that irked her. She did not need a man to touch her. If only she could find a man who wanted a woman to work with him, sort of in a business way, then she would go. And three days later she saw it:

Christian widower seeks mother for his two daughters.

My name is William Edwards and I am a widower aged thirty years. I have two daughters, aged ten and twelve years. I am a rancher in Missoula, Montana. We attend the Missoula Baptist Church under Pastor Thomas Clifford. I am looking for a Christian woman to marry and be a mother to my daughters. She should be between nineteen to twenty-one years old. A widow with children is also welcome. Send me a letter if you are interested, and I promise to reply.

Elizabeth looked at the advert and when Virginia was asleep, she knelt down beside the bed.

"Father, I am your child and you know my needs and my desires and my suffering. Matilda told me about finding a husband from the west, and today when I went and bought the paper I found this advert by Mr. William Edwards. He sounds like a fine man who will not place too many unnecessary demands on me. If it is in your will, let my letter reach him and let me find favor in his eyes. You know the hearts of all men and Lord, if you have looked into the heart of Mr. William Edwards and seen a kind man, then I pray that you allow this process to go speedily, because I have to take Virginia out of this place before she loses her soul. In Jesus' name, amen."

CHAPTER TWO

MISSOULA, MONTANA
EARLY SPRING, 1874

"Amelia, why did you have to leave me?" William Edwards, a tall muscular man, stood, hat in hand with his head bowed as his tears dropped onto the grave at his feet. It was a well-tended grave that made all who saw it aware that whoever lay beneath the earth had been well loved.

The tombstone read:

Here lies

Amelia Jane Edwards

1845 - 1873

Beloved Wife and Mother

Rest in Peace.

William wrung his leather hat in his large hands.

"I am sorry I let you down," he sobbed. "I am so sorry."

William knelt at the foot of the grave, uncaring that the earth was still wet from an early morning drizzle. He had come here every morning for the last year since he had buried his wife of thirteen years.

Amelia had been a fine young lady of sixteen when they had met. He was eighteen, and for him it was love at first sight.

They had met in church at a wedding. Amelia's family had just moved to Missoula from Helena. Her father had been a prospective miner, but when he and his wife and daughter had reached Helena, he had quickly realized that mining was not what he wanted to do, and he had responded to the government's Homestead Act, which offered one hundred and sixty acres of land to the head of a family, or any citizen twenty-one years or older, and because women were also allowed to apply for the land, Reginald and Miriam Willoughby had both applied and jointly got three hundred and twenty acres of land.

They were strong Christians and their daughter, Amelia, was a very pretty girl. Just a few months after they moved to Missoula, Reginald and Miriam had been killed in a storm. Amelia had been at Pastor Thomas' house, preparing for Sunday school because she taught the young ones, and so had not been at home when the house fell on her sleeping parents and killed them instantly.

For a long time Amelia had grieved for her parents, but Pastor Thomas, his wife Salome, and other members of the congregation had supported her, most of all William, who had seen to the settlement of the Willoughby's estate. Most of the money went to repaying her father's debts, as the farm had not started producing anything, and he had borrowed large sums to develop it.

Amelia eventually also fell in love with William, and after courting for two months they were married and settled down on William's one hundred and sixty acre farm.

William lived with his sister, Katherine, who was then thirteen years old. William had inherited his father's farm when the latter ran off with a saloon lady, leaving their mother quite devastated, and she had pined away and died.

Life for William and his new wife Amelia had been full of joy as they brought their children into the world. The two loved each other deeply, and Amelia was a very strong woman who was rarely ill.

So when William had returned from one of his hunts for mustangs to add to his horse ranch and found her lying in bed, he was not overly concerned.

"Feeling a little under the weather," Amelia had said. "It is just a cold, nothing to worry about." But that night she took a turn for the worse, and by the time William rode in the early dawn to get the local doctor and returned, Amelia's breathing was raspy and quite labored.

"Why didn't you get me earlier?" Dr. Shawn had asked him, frowning deeply. "Your wife has influenza, and it seems to have spread to her lungs."

"Please do all you can to help my Amelia get better," William had begged.

But in the end, Amelia had lost the fight.

Now, standing beside her grave, all William had to give his wife was tears. "I am sorry I let you down, Amelia," he wept. Though he felt like he might never stop missing her, never stop grieving, he never wanted his daughters to know the depth of his pain. He had to be strong for them as they struggled to go on with their lives after the loss of their mother. He could not add to his children's pain.

At least, William could tell his wife that he was doing well by their children. "Amelia, your daughters are growing into fine young women. Mary is looking more and more like you every day, and it hurts when I look into her eyes and see you staring back at me." He shook his head. "I miss you greatly, Amelia. I miss you so much." The pain in his heart threatened to overwhelm him. "I promise I will never love another woman like I loved you. I will devote my life to looking after our girls." He wiped his nose on the back of his hand. Then he wiped his hand on his black dungarees. "Abigail is turning into an expert horse rider, like you were. You would be proud of the girls, Amelia." He sniffed. "Why did you have to leave us? How do I go on without you? The girls are getting to the age when they need a woman. They need you, Amelia. Why did you leave us?"

Tired of kneeling, he sat down and began plucking the small weeds that had begun forming on the grave. He worked silently for a while.

William was not worried about his children. His sister Katherine had come from her home in Butte to check on them as she did every two months since Amelia had died, and whenever she came, at least the house and their clothes got a good washing. She would come in with strong detergent and coax the girls into helping her clean the cabin from top to bottom.

He was on a short break before he went back to the mountains to meet Sure Foot, his good Nez Perce Indian friend who had taught him how to track and chase after mustangs. He had discovered that dealing in horses was better than dealing in cattle because for one, the mustangs were wild creatures that could be allowed back into the wild during winter to forage for themselves, and come spring he could go back and recapture them and sell them to the many miners who transited through Missoula for lands beyond, in search of gold, silver and copper. And besides, the mustangs were strong riding horses, and the stage coach owners preferred them to other breeds because they were hardy animals and could endure adverse situations and weather.

Keeping horses had proved profitable to William, and though he was by no means rich he managed to give his family a comfortable life. But life without a wife was quite a challenge.

After a long while he stood up and looked at his handiwork. Amelia's grave looked fresh and pretty from the flowers that he had picked on his way up there. He kissed the tombstone and then turned homeward.

~~~ *** ~~~

"Abigail, where are you?" Katherine called in exasperation. The child could be trying at times. "Where are you at?"

"Auntie Kate, I am going to feed Misty and Spitfire and Primrose," Abigail called out.

Katherine sighed. Her brother's children were a strange lot, and she knew that if she did not work so hard to visit every two months, they would slowly turn into vagabonds because their father seemed to be lost in a world of his own since his wife's death.

"What these girls need is a mother," Katherine muttered as she aired the girls' bedroom. Her brown hair was neatly wrapped in a headscarf as she worked, her plump body shaking with exertion. Her nieces worried her greatly. They were growing up very fast, and she was fearful that without a woman to guide them they might fall prey to the wranglers who frequented the ranch from time to time in search of work.

William's ranch was mostly wild ground because he allowed his horses freedom to roam the property. But he also had a few head of cattle, and Amelia had kept some chickens and goats. The number had dwindled after her death, but she could see that Mary was trying to keep her mother's dream of having a self-sufficient farm alive. But the girl was only a child. Whenever the grass was tall William would look for wranglers to come and help him cut it to make hay for his animals.

Katherine sighed, her blue eyes quite troubled. She finished making the girls' beds, left their bedroom and walked to the kitchen, wondering where Mary was. She had allowed her brother to grieve for his wife, but four months after her death she had tried to broach the subject of him getting another wife, and almost got her head bitten off for her efforts.

"We are alright," William had snapped at her. "If you are tired of coming to check on us then stay at home with your husband and children. We do not want to be a bother to you."

At the time Kate had put it down to grief and excused her brother's behavior. But now, a year later, he was still not showing any signs of moving on. She knew that he visited Amelia's grave every morning when he was home, and she felt that it was becoming an obsession with him. She realized that she would have to use tough love to wake her brother up, or else he would lose his children. William was like their mother, very soft-hearted, and when their father had run off with another woman, Brigitte had slowly given up the will to live and one day they had found her dead in her bed.

When Kate heard Abigail laughing happily, she knew her brother had returned from his morning ritual at Amelia's graveside. She heard the ten year old chattering and her father responding, and soon the back door opened.

"Good day." William entered the kitchen.

"Hello, William," she smiled at him. "How was your morning ride?"

"Refreshing." He pulled out a chair at the round table and sat down, and Abigail immediately sat on his lap. He ruffled her hair. It was brown, like his.

"Why did you cut your hair again, Abigail?" her aunt asked her. The child turned her blue eyes, so much like her father's, and looked at her aunt.

"It is too heavy, and besides, when I ride the horses and the wind blows, it gets in my eyes."

Kate sighed inwardly. That girl was a trial and a growing one. "Where is Mary? Go and fetch her so we can have lunch together. I need to have an early start back home today. The stagecoach should be at Hellgate at around four, and I do not want to miss it."

William raised his tanned face to his sister. "You promised you would stay until Saturday, and it is only Wednesday."

Kate twisted her lips. "I know, but I think I have to leave."

Mary walked in at that moment and heard her aunt saying that she wanted to leave, and she rushed to her.

"Aunt Kate, please don't go," she hugged the surprised woman. "I will be good. Please don't go today. Promise that you will stay." Her large brown eyes held fear and sadness, and now welled with tears as she looked pleadingly at her aunt.

"Okay, okay," Kate laughingly extracted herself from the girl's thin hands. Her brown hair was messed up, and Kate sighed. She could never get it to look neat, much as she combed it. Her usual style was a thick braid that Kate did her best to comb out whenever she could, in order to avoid the child getting head lice.

Mary was becoming clingy and Kate realized this was not a good sign. She would serve lunch, and when the girls were done eating she would send them off on an errand and have a heart-to-heart talk with her brother.

"William," she said, after the girls had left for Pastor Thomas' home just a few miles away on the ridge.

"Yes?"

"I want you to listen to me," Katherine said in a quiet voice, and something in her tone made William look at her sharply.

"What is it?"

"It is about Abby and Mary. I love those girls and you know it, but I cannot take the place of their mother, William."

"No one can ever take Amelia's place."

"I know that. But what I mean is that they need a woman full-time, and I can only be here every other month at most. My own family needs me, and it is becoming increasingly difficult for me to keep coming over, especially since Marshall was voted-in as sheriff of Butte."

"I am sorry that we have imposed so much on your time."

She shook her head. "That is not what I am saying, William." She sighed. "What I mean is that the girls are growing up fast, and before you know it, boys and men will be beating a path to your doorstep. Are you ready for that to happen?"

"No," William growled. "I will kill any man who dares show his face around here."

"You cannot stop the river from flowing, and so you need to be prepared for when that happens. Mary is turning out to be a beautiful young lady, and I am getting quite disturbed."

"Why?"

"You are not around much, and even when you are, you seem to be lost in a world of your own. Have you noticed that the wranglers, who come in search of work, tend to hang around long after the work is over, on pretext of one thing or the other?"

"What?"

Kate nodded. "I am getting worried, because without proper monitoring one of those boys will 'convince' Mary, and take advantage of her."

William put his head in his hands and looked down. "What do I do? I cannot stay here all day to look after Mary! And when I am away, Mrs. Thomas comes to look after the girls."

"But do you see what an inconvenience that is? She has to leave Pastor Thomas, and the children, and come to take on extra work."

"What do you want me to do?"

"Get a wife," Katherine held up a hand when he would have spoken. "I know you loved Amelia so much, no one can ever doubt that. But you have got to consider that the children now need a mother, and someone to be here full-time for them."

"We are doing alright."

"No, William. You are trying to convince yourself of that fact, but you also know that what I am saying is true. Besides, the girls are at a very sensitive stage, and on the threshold of turning into young women. Who do you want to help them transition? A new mother? Or the wranglers who come here?"

"Don't say that."

"I have to. You need to face reality. It is not easy, and I am not saying you jump on just any woman, but please, think about what I am telling you."

"But Kate, all the good ladies I know are married. And those who are not married are not the kind that I want around my girls."

"Then let me help you get a wife."

"Where from?"

"Mail order."

"What?" William hooted with laughter. "Are you serious?"

"Yes, William. Many of the ladies who live around here have acquired a certain class because of the exposure to miners and wealth, and so they have extreme demands. And besides, many of them are not even Christians. But think about the ladies who come west to be brides. They are women who are serious about building their own homes, and that is why they would risk leaving everything behind to come to the Wild West."

William was shaking his head in amusement. "Have you heard of anyone ordering for a bride through the mail?"

"In Butte, yes," Katherine nodded. "It happens all the time. And the women are hard-working and soon settle down and become good farmers' wives and mothers."

Later that night as William lay on his bed, he thought about what his sister had told him. What she said made perfect sense, but he could not imagine another woman coming into his life, into his house, and into the bed which he had shared with Amelia. He could not imagine getting intimate with any other woman. He put his hands behind his head and stared at the ceiling in the darkness. He heard murmurs and realized that his sister and daughters were not yet asleep.

He listened and heard sniffles, and knew that one of his daughters was crying again. He sighed and got out of bed to go and find out what was going on. He opened the door and walked barefoot, his feet making no sound on the wooden floor. When he got to the girls' room the door was slightly ajar, and he could see Kate sitting on Mary's bed. The little girl was in her aunt's arms for a while, and then she sat back.

"Aunt Kate, why can't you be our mother?"

"Because dear, I have a family of my own, and I can only be your aunt."

"Why can't you talk to Papa to get us a new mom? All the other children have mothers.

We don't."

"I know, child, I know. Give your father time, and he will soon get you a mother."

"When?" she demanded. "Even Betsy's father married another mother for them when their mother died, and now they have a mother. Why can't we have a mother?"

"Your pa will soon get you a mother," Kate said, but there was doubt in her voice.

"It is okay, aunty. Because Pa is shy, I have already started looking for a wife for him."

"What?"

"I will find a mother for Abigail and me, and a wife for Pa."

"Where from, child?"

"Mrs. Thomas said if I put an advert in the newspaper, some woman from the east is bound to be looking for a husband and will reply, and she can come here and be our mom. So I asked Daddy for some money, went with Mrs. Thomas to town in Hellgate, and placed an advert. The kind man said he will run it and send it to different newspapers in different cities, so that Papa can get a wife quickly."

"Oh, child."

William went back to his room and flung himself on the bed, face down. Now his daughter too? He groaned silently. Why couldn't everyone leave him alone? He loved Amelia and there was no room in his heart for another woman. Pastor Thomas had been visiting every week since Amelia died, and lately he and his wife had been hinting at the same thing. It was as though everyone was conspiring against him. He fumed silently.

"I won't be forced into marriage," he gritted through his teeth. "They have to realize that I am not interested."

But in the morning, when William looked at his children and especially Mary, compassion welled up in his heart. As usual, Mary was the one who set the table for meals, and as usual she took her mother's coffee mug out of the cabinet and set it on the table. But then as usual, she did not use it, nor did she put anything in it, and once again at the end of the meal she put it back in the cabinet.

Katherine was observing her brother as he observed his daughter, and when he realized she was staring at him, he looked up. Her eyes were pleading with him. He nodded and she smiled.

His daughter's actions were not normal for a twelve-year-old girl, and he realized that, much as he did not want to, he was going to make some changes in his household and find a mother for his girls.

As he walked out to feed the horses Abigail skipped happily beside him. She seemed to cling to him more, and he realized that whenever he was around she was very happy, but the moment he mentioned that he had to go to the mountains she would weep and pout and cling. Mrs. Thomas had told him that she refused to join other children and preferred being with the horses. By nature, Mary was the clingy one, but he realized that Abigail had begun clinging to him and staying very close to him.

"Pa?"

"Yes, Abby?"

"Will you ever leave us?"

William stopped abruptly and she bumped into him. He wheeled around to look at her.

"What?"

"Will you go away to the mountains, and not come back again one day?"

He crouched until he was on eye level with the little girl.

"Why would you think that?"

"Because, you are always so sad after Ma died, and Aunt Kate said you were pining so much, and might fade away."

William kissed his daughter's forehead. "Your pa is here to stay with you, okay?"

"Pa?"

"Yes?"

"Will you take me with you to the mountains?"

"Abby, we have talked about this. Besides, who will stay with Mary if we both go?"

Abigail sighed. "If we had a ma, she could stay with Mary, and then I could come with you to the mountains to catch horses."

~~~ *** ~~~

The girls were asleep, but William was wide awake. He sat on the porch and wished he could smoke his pipe, but it was a habit he had given up when he married Amelia. He just kept the pipe to remind him of days gone by.

The moon was new and gave some light, and he sat deep in thought. The stagecoach had come to Hellgate while he was there escorting Kate to return home, and the driver, who knew him very well, had given him a letter. It was from a woman in New York who had seen his advert and had responded. According to the letter she was twenty-two years old and a widow. Her husband had died three years previously, leaving her with two young sons to raise, and now life in New York was proving very tough. She mentioned that she was a hard worker and was ready to get more children, something which had made William shudder. He could not imagine holding any other woman in his arms. It would be a deep betrayal to Amelia. This was definitely not the kind of woman he wanted, but out of courtesy he sent her a letter requesting her to share more information about her and her expectations for life as a settler's wife.

Over the next week four more letters came for William, and he straight away discarded two of them. The women were sixteen years old, only a few years older than his own daughters. He did not need another child to look after. He wanted a mother for Mary and Abigail.

He pondered the remaining two. One was from a woman in Chicago who was twenty and had never been married, neither did she have any children. William shook his head at this one, too. She wanted children, but he was not interested in the intimacy side of the marriage. But just like with the first woman, he sent her a letter asking her to give her expectations as a frontier wife.

The last letter had him thinking deeply.

Dear Mr. William Edwards,

My name is Elizabeth Anne Lowell and I am nineteen years old. I am a Christian, and belong to the Boston Baptist Church. I read your advert in the Boston Daily and realize that you are the kind of man that I am hoping to meet and marry. My sister, Virginia, who is fifteen years old, and I are orphans. Mama died when I was nine and Virginia was six, and Papa died two months ago, leaving us all alone in the world.

I am well-educated because Papa engaged the services of an English school madam for us. I play the violin very well, as I was taught by an Italian immigrant. I can also cook very well and clean the house. Besides that, my nanny Ruth also taught me how to make soap and oils, and I know that these are items that many frontier wives have need for, and so when it comes to the matter of upkeep, I will easily make money to fend for Virginia and myself.

As this is the first letter, I do not want to write too much for fear of being thought a chatterer. Let me mention that I wear glasses, especially to read with. I hope this will not make you think that I am blind and cannot make a good settler's wife. Most days I do not wear them because I can see alright. However, when I need to read, then I put them on.

Having said all this, if my letter meets with your favor I will be glad to receive a response from you.

Elizabeth.

William thought about this letter deeply. The woman did not mention children anywhere. And she talked of going into business for herself. This sounded like a woman who was very independent, and perhaps they could come to an agreement. He frowned. But he would not be quick to accept her. She might just get here and begin to demand her conjugal rights.

"I will test and see if this woman is the kind that I am looking for." So he wrote back and asked her how many children she thought they should have together, should they get married. Her answer surprised him and brought a smile to his face.

Dear Mr. William Edwards,

Thank you for responding to my letter. I am most touched that you thought of asking about our welfare. We live in a rooming house, and I work for the landlady as a scullery maid. In return, we have the room rent-free and she gives us two meals a day.

Regarding the matter of children, I believe your advert said you already have two children and I feel that there is no need to add more, at least not at this point in time. Mary and Abigail are at an age where they need a mother, probably more than you need a wife, and so it would be better to hold off thinking about children until the girls are established and settled in their new life with a new mother. I have been reading up a little on life on the frontier, as written by early settlers' wives, and it seems like hard work, which I of course will be glad to do. However, that will probably not leave any room for children, because you told me that your ranch is still small and you are working to make it bigger and more productive. Therefore, what I am saying is that I am begging your pardon, but should you and I get married, can we hold off having more children for another five years?

Most kindly,

Elizabeth.

William smiled. This might just work out. The woman did not seem interested in intimacy. Five years? Which man and woman can live together and not have children within five years, unless one of them was barren? In his case he was not, and he wondered whether Elizabeth was barren and was probably just using that as an excuse.

The other two women had responded and he immediately realized that they thought he was a rich land owner, with a large sprawling mansion where they would entertain widely. In their own different ways each of them wanted to know which clothes would be suitable for them as the ladies of the house, and if he could finance their *trousseaus* as they prepared to come out west.

With a sigh he wrote back his regrets to the two ladies, explaining that his ranch was only one hundred and sixty acres and his house was made of logs and sod, and since he was still in mourning there would not be any entertainment at the homestead for many years to come.

He still had one further test to do before he made up his mind about Elizabeth. He sent her another letter requesting references from her pastor with regards to her virtue.

Dear Mr. William Edwards,

Once again it was a pleasure to read your letter. From the time I was small my parents, and especially Mama, took us to church and when I turned twelve I was baptized by the Reverend Isaiah Banks of the Boston Baptist Church. We have attended the same church all our lives, and Rev. Banks can vouch for my virtue. I have never been married before, nor have I known a man in the Biblical sense of the word, nor do I have the wish to do so in the near future. I realize this may compromise my position as an applicant for the state of marriage with you, but I am being totally honest. For the time being, I believe we will have a lot of work to do on the ranch so as not to leave room for any intimacies. Besides, my desire is to find a home for my sister, Virginia, who has been very sick, and the doctor said that I need to get her out of this cold Boston climate to a warmer place where she can recuperate and once again be healthy.

In view of this, I would like to ask you to agree to a business arrangement where I promise to look after your children and your household, and in return you provide me with a name and a roof over our heads, because two women alone in a strange land would create a lot of problems.

I will be waiting to hear back from you. However, if I do not hear from you within the month, I will take it that my request has not met with your approval and so will look elsewhere.

I am also enclosing a reference from Reverend Isaiah Banks with regard to our standing in the church.

Thank you most kindly.

Elizabeth Lowell.

This last letter decided the matter for him, and when he next wrote he enclosed twenty dollars which he took from his savings for their train and coach transportation, together with detailed information on how they could get to Missoula.

CHAPTER THREE

FARGO, NORTH DAKOTA
SPRING, 1874

Elizabeth stepped onto the platform of the railway station at Fargo and stretched. She put her glasses back in their case, because she did not need them now that she was not reading any more. Her whole body was sore from sitting through seven days of the train journey. She had given up her seat from time to time so that Virginia, who was still recuperating, could stretch out more. Being a tall girl did not help and Virginia had been grumpy most of the way. Elizabeth put it down to the effects of her illness and so did not take offence, not even when her sister was sometimes downright rude to her.

"I never wanted to come on this horrible journey to a forsaken country," she sniffed at one point. "Why did you have to take me away from all that is dear to me?"

"Virginia, the doctor said you need fresh air and lots of warmth in order for the inflammation to heal. Boston is not the place, and Missoula will be good for you. The fresh mountain air will do you lots of good."

"You don't know that," she cried shrilly. "Why must you always decide things for me, even when I do not want you to? Is it because you are jealous of me? I am prettier, and you know that in Boston I would have soon found a good man to pay me suit. Why, oh why, did you have to take me away?"

Elizabeth chose to ignore her sister's taunt and instead looked out of the window. However, as they neared Fargo Virginia's countenance had begun to change into a pleasant one, and Elizabeth hoped the sullen mood had passed, at least for now. This was the last train station, and from here they would use the stagecoach to Missoula, and William would meet them at the Missoula Travelers' Inn.

In the days leading up to their departure from Boston, she had sought to find out as much information as she could regarding their journey to the Wild West. Having never ventured out of Boston she had been both thrilled and frightened of the unknown, but days spent in prayer gave her the calm she needed.

"Isn't there a train right up to Missoula?" she had inquired at the station, and the elderly station master had smiled at her indulgently.

"Miss, I know for a fact that if you were to take this journey in another five year, then the train will convey you right up to your destination in Missoula. But alas! For now, the Northern Pacific rail tracks have only been laid as far as Fargo in North Dakota."

"How long will the journey last? I mean from here up to North Dakota?"

"If God permits it, then you can be sure that in eight days from when you board the train you will be in Fargo. Then you take the stagecoach from there. If you are lucky, it may pass right outside your destination, but if not then you will be put down at Missoula Travelers' Inn." Elizabeth had smiled since that is what William had indicated in his letter. He would be waiting for them. At least she prayed that he was a man of integrity and would be waiting for them. Now, as she helped Virginia off the train she looked around to see if she could find a seat. She still had to get their portmanteau which contained all their worldly possessions, as well as her violin.

She spotted a small stone slab and led her sister to it. The girl began grumbling once again.

"Ginnie, I have to get our luggage. You will be alright here." She hurried back to the train and brought down their luggage and carried it to where she had left Virginia. She straightened herself and looked around. They had reached Fargo in the early morning on a Thursday, or at least she hoped it was Thursday, because she had listened in on a conversation between two elderly men, and had understood that as they travelled further West they were losing time. She had no idea what losing time was and hoped to find someone to explain it all her.

There was the usual railway station hustle and bustle as people met relatives and exchanged excited greetings. She watched in fascination as various activities went on around them. Then she heard the sound she had been listening out for.

"Stagecoach to Fort Benton, Sun River, Fort Shaw, Helena, Missoula. Stagecoach to Fort Benton, Sun River, Fort Shaw, Helena, Missoula. Get your seat now," the shrill crier's voice rang out.

"That is our coach, Virginia. Let us go."

Virginia stood up and began walking ahead, not offering to help her sister with the luggage, and Elizabeth struggled with the portmanteau and violin case and was thankful when she reached the outside of the station. She looked around and spotted Virginia standing beside the coach, observing the horses. There were about three coaches and were each drawn by four large horses.

Elizabeth had never seen a horse up close, and she was fascinated as well as terrified of them. She hoped they were not temperamental creatures and as she handed their luggage over to the driver of their coach she made a silent prayer.

"We have come this far because of Your protection, Lord, but our journey is not yet over. Guide us through this vast land, and help us reach our destination. In Jesus' name, amen." She climbed in and sat beside Virginia, who had taken the window seat.

Elizabeth looked around the coach with a lot of interest and smiled at a woman her own age who had two children with her, a little boy and a little girl. The woman smiled back at her. Their coach soon filled and in total there were eight of them, five ladies and three gentlemen, besides the two children. They sat on hard seats, four on each side facing each other. The driver came to the door. Elizabeth offered to hold the little boy and his mother gladly handed the child over.

"Ladies and gentlemen, welcome to Wells Fargo Stage Coach. My name is Jack Sprat. Our first stop will be at Glitch. Between Fargo and Fort Benton we will make very short stops, because most of the towns along the way are very small, and staying too long might attract the wrong kind of attention. As all three coaches will be riding together, we shall also make the journey at night. That will ensure triple security for all of us." He looked at all his passengers. "But there is nothing to worry about. Once we get to Fort Benton you can enjoy the view from there, because our pace will be a little bit more leisurely. Once again, welcome to Wells Fargo Stage Coach and have a good journey."

True to his word Jack, as well as the other coach drivers, rode the horses hard and between Fargo and Fort Benton they only stopped a few times to change horses. Everything flew past like a blur, and because the seats were very uncomfortable and the ride a bumpy one, the passengers were more concerned with staying on their seats than on viewing the landscape.

When they got to Fort Benton six days later, things changed. Jack took the weary travelers to a courtyard inn which looked very comfortable.

"This is my sister's place," he grinned as he helped the tired ladies out of the coach. A plump matronly woman with a bonnet on her head emerged from the building, a huge smile on her face.

"Hello brother, it is good to see you indeed," she hugged her brother, who turned to introduce his passengers. "Jack, show the gentlemen to their rooms and I will make the ladies comfortable."

Elizabeth was glad to sleep on a bed that night, even if she had to share it with Virginia, who tossed and turned the whole night.

"We will soon be there," Elizabeth soothed her murmuring sister. "I am sorry you have to endure all this discomfort, but it will soon be over. Mr. Jack said we are about seven days away from our destination."

"Why did we have to come at all?"

Elizabeth ignored her sister and pretended to fall asleep. As she lay in the darkness it suddenly came to her that she had to think about their lives ahead. When she had received the letter with the money for transport for both of them from William, her only thought had been to get her sister out of Boston, away from the bad influence of the city and to a place where she could be safe. She had not given herself time to think about the forthcoming marriage.

She had told William that she wanted a marriage in name only, but what if when they got there he wanted a real marriage and children? She shuddered. The thought of a man touching her made her recoil inwardly.

Elizabeth knew she was not a prude, but growing up in Boston and being around the servants and especially after her mother had died, had left a negative picture about the relations between men and women. Perhaps if her mother had been alive she might have given Elizabeth the proper education regarding marriage and marital relations, but whatever she knew she had learned from the servants' whispers and giggles. And it made her abhor intimacy because the servants made it sound like an evil act.

"Please, Lord, let William not be a man who has those carnal needs," she prayed silently. "Let him be an honorable man, who needs only a mother for his children and nothing more."

They left at dawn the next day and this time, because they were in what Jack Sprat called the 'Gold Country,' there was a lot of traffic on the road and their journey was more leisurely. Elizabeth saw the tall prairie grass rippling like the waves of the sea in the breeze, and animals and rocks dotted the land, which was green all over since it was early spring. This land was untouched and unsoiled, a wilderness that overwhelmed and made Elizabeth feel very small and vulnerable.

When they rolled into Missoula at last, almost three weeks to the day that they had started their journey west, Elizabeth's heart began to pound in her chest. This was it. She was really here, actually here to get married. She had no idea what her husband-to-be looked like, but he had mentioned that he was six feet and two inches tall.

Nothing however, prepared her for the first sight of the man she was to be married to. As she stepped out of the coach something told her to look towards her left and she saw a mountain of a man, with dark brown hair, a square jaw and piercing blue eyes. It was the eyes that held her captive. Very beautiful but sad eyes. He blinked and turned away, breaking their eye contact. Elizabeth knew without being told that this was William.

He strode over to the coach and after exchanging pleasantries with Jack, he turned to her. "You must be Elizabeth Anne Lowell. Welcome to Missoula, Montana, ma'am," he took off his hat. "And this must be your sister, Virginia." He had a deep and pleasant voice.

He held out his hand and Elizabeth placed hers in it. He had rough hands, the hands of a man who worked hard. William was thinking the same thing about Elizabeth. Her hands were not the soft hands of someone who had been indulged. And they were stained with blue marks, which he correctly presumed to be ink stains. She had mentioned that she was a transcriber. He greeted Virginia, who flashed a smile at him.

"Where is your luggage?" he asked, and Elizabeth indicated the portmanteau which he picked up easily, leaving Elizabeth to carry her violin.

Elizabeth was expecting to see a coach of some sort or an ox wagon, and the sight of the three horses standing side by side and to which William strode made her falter in her steps.

"Anything wrong, ma'am?"

"Are those horses?" she asked, and then cleared her throat. "I mean, are we supposed to ride those horses?" She spoke to him for the first time and he thought she had a very musical voice.

"Yes, ma'am."

"But I, we have never ridden on a horse before," she said in almost a whisper. She was terrified and it showed in her large eyes. She was afraid that Virginia would burst into tears, but was quite surprised when the young girl walked up to one of the horses and began stroking the animal, which seemed to like what she was doing.

"It is not difficult, ma'am. Besides the horses will get us faster to wherever we are going."

"What?" Elizabeth's heart sank. When she had been preparing for their journey she had been fully aware that they were going into the wilderness, but she had hoped that it would be a civilized environment.

William's heart sank. Surely the woman was not going to bail out on him at this point! He did not want to go through the ordeal of corresponding with any more women. This first time had been hard enough as it was.

"Are you changing your mind, ma'am?" he spoke softly so that only she heard, and she heard the challenging tone in his deep voice.

"No, of course not." She sighed. "But …" she shrugged and turned away. "Never mind." William put the portmanteau down and scratched his chin, which showed signs of a beard.

"Riding a horse is not that difficult, and you will soon get the hang of it."

Elizabeth had her doubts but she squared her shoulders and prepared herself to face whatever lay ahead.

"Here, I will help you up. You can have Misty. She is a very gently one and has never thrown anyone."

"Thrown anyone?"

"Horses tend to sense fear, and if you get on a horse and it senses your fears it can easily throw you off. Not with Misty. My daughters learned how to ride on her."

He looked at her and Virginia and shook his head.

"What now?" Elizabeth demanded.

"You have to ride side-saddle, because you are not properly dressed for riding astride."

"What does that mean?"

"Your dresses will not allow you to ride while seated astride," he pointed at a cowboy who was passing by on his horse. His legs were on either side of his horse. "That is what riding astride means."

"Oh, I see," Elizabeth said. She threw a quick glance at Virginia, who was still petting her horse.

"Your sister seems quite at home with animals. Are you sure she has never ridden before?"

"No, sir," Elizabeth murmured.

"Before you get on Misty you need to make her acquaintance. Horses are like people sometimes. They are temperamental creatures, and if she knows you are a friend you will not have any problems with her." Elizabeth was standing about five feet away from the horse. William held out his hand. "Come and meet Misty."

She put down her violin case and reluctantly placed her hand in his, and he tugged at it gently and she followed him. He stood before the horse's head and pulled her to stand alongside him.

Misty was black and had a white stripe from her ears down her muzzle. The other two horses were pure black all over.

"Touch her muzzle," he said in a soft voice. "Misty likes that."

"No!" Elizabeth tried to pull her hand away but he held on firm.

"You are a very brave woman, Miss Elizabeth," he said without looking at her, stroking Misty with his left hand. "You left all your life behind to come into the unknown. A horse is a very small thing to beat you now."

Elizabeth inwardly agreed with what he was saying. She sighed and allowed him to place her hand on the horse's muzzle. She was surprised at how soft it felt.

"She is so soft," she said in wonder, stepping a little bit closer.

Misty breathed onto her hand and she could not hide a giggle, and her dimples showed, lighting up her expressive eyes, and William caught his breath. She was very beautiful and he quickly quashed the thought.

"Hello, Misty," Elizabeth, a little braver, reached both hands and cupped the horse's head. "You are a very beautiful one." The horse made a sound as if she fully agreed with what Elizabeth was saying, and she giggled again.

"Misty is female, so she loves the compliments," William said. The woman would be alright. He had a more pressing issue. The portmanteau, though not heavy, was nevertheless bulky and he was thinking about how to tie it and the violin onto Black Thunder, his horse. He scratched his chin again and sighed. Women, he thought, and their possessions. He remembered that when they had migrated from Texas to Montana before the Civil War, he and his father only had saddle bags but his mother had to have all her possessions with her. With the use of ropes he managed to secure the luggage and then he turned first to Virginia.

"Need any help getting on?" he asked her.

"A little, I guess," she laughed briefly. "What is this horse's name?"

"That is Spitfire. She is a strong willed one, but you seem to have befriended her."

"She is very pretty." William hoisted Virginia effortlessly onto the horse, and was surprised when she ignored all propriety and sat astride the horse. He shook his head. This was a spirited one, just like the horse. They should be fine together. The other one, his wife-to-be, was the problem.

"Miss Elizabeth?"

"Yes, Mr. William?"

"Your turn now. Misty will not throw you. Just hold onto the reins and do not pull. Just hold them gently and we should get there."

"How far do we have to ride?"

"About a two-hour ride. I will take it slow, but we need to leave if we are to get home before nightfall."

"Okay," she said. But she was murmuring a prayer. "I can do all things through Christ which strengthens me. Lord, please help me not to fall off the horse."

William lifted the woman off the ground. "Don't look down. Concentrate on looking at Misty's head, and you will be fine," he said. Elizabeth sat side-saddle and clutched the reins, startling Misty, who shifted nervously.

"Hush, lady," William quickly pacified her and she calmed down. He put his hands over Elizabeth's. "You need to relax, or you will spook Misty. Loosen your grip a little bit, there, that should be alright now."

He walked to Black Thunder. "All ready now?"

"Yes," Virginia shouted, sounding like an excited child.

William looked at his betrothed, who nodded, too afraid to speak. He got onto his horse effortlessly and Elizabeth admired his agility. He made a clicking sound and Spitfire, with Virginia on her back, set off and took a side trail.

"I am avoiding the town center," he said. "It does no good to draw people's attention to oneself," he explained. "Spitfire knows the way home, and that is why I want her to lead the way. Elizabeth, you will go before me so that I can watch you."

"Thank you," she said quietly. "What is the name of this town? Is this Missoula?"

"Well, Missoula is the whole county. This particular town is called Hellgate."

"Why such a sinister name?"

"That is what the pioneers called this place, when they first came here years ago. It is said that they found skulls and bones of people scattered all over."

"Who had killed the people? What had happened to them?"

"The Blackfeet and Flatfeet Indians used this as a fighting field, or so the legend goes. It is not a bad town, but you would do well to keep away and avoid it altogether, especially when it is dark."

"Oh."

"Gold attracts all kinds: the good, the bad, and the ugly. In Hellgate there are many good folks, but the ugly are here, too."

William chatted to Elizabeth, pointing out various plants and trees to her as they rode through the woods. She soon forgot her nervousness and began enjoying the ride.

"Almost home," he said, and she spied a clearing just ahead of where he pointed. Virginia was happily trotting on her horse ahead of the two of them. And then they broke out of the woods and Elizabeth gasped.

"Are you alright, Miss Elizabeth?" William was immediately concerned when he saw her expression. Her mouth opened and closed several times, and tears welled up in her eyes.

"Oh Lord, my God, how majestic is Your name in all the earth," Elizabeth whispered, too awed by what she saw ahead of her. The mountain range rose majestically in the distance and the air had suddenly become cool and clear. The afternoon sun made the peaks seem like they were on fire. The blue sky above the mountains was clear and she saw dots of white on the peaks. This was God's country. This was the splendor of God, His beauty in creation, and Elizabeth's tears fell as she pondered the majesty of the Creator of the universe.

"You made the mountains," she whispered. "How awesome and terrible You are."

Even Misty sensed the reverence of the moment and came to a gentle halt, an unspoken command that only animal and nature understood together. Elizabeth slowly raised her hands as if in surrender and closed her eyes, oblivious to all around her, just the beauty that she had witnessed. Her life would never be the same again after this, she knew. She opened her eyes again and then lowered her hands and smiled. She had heard about the Rocky Mountains from her father and tutor, but nothing had prepared her for this glorious sight.

"Thank you, Lord. Thank you, Jesus, for allowing me to live long enough to see the splendor of Your majesty in creation. For as long as I live, I will praise You and worship You, for You alone are God."

William watched his betrothed's face in fascination. That she loved God was all too clear to him at that point, and he shifted uncomfortably in his saddle. She made him feel guilty and he did not want to analyze his feelings any deeper, for fear of what he would find. He had turned his back on God, and any form of worship, after Amelia died. If God was so loving, why had He allowed a young mother with so many dreams and a future to die, and leave behind a widower with two small children? What kind of God did that to those who served Him? Despite the fact that his father had run off years ago and left his mother, his mother had been a deeply religious woman, and she had taught her children the fear of the Lord.

Katherine loved church and she attended all services faithfully, and had tried to convince her brother to return. Pastor Thomas also visited him from time to time, urging him to return to the fold, but he stubbornly refused to yield.

"God is waiting for you, William," Kate told him on many

occasions. "Do not give up on God. He has not given up on you."

"Well, He did, when He let Amelia die. What kind of God causes those He claims to love so much pain?" was all he usually said whenever Katherine or Pastor Thomas tried to ask him to go to church. Because he stopped going to church, his daughters also did not attend Sunday school. And now here was this woman, obviously of deep faith. What did that mean to his peace of mind, and his household?

"We need to leave," he said, more gruffly than he intended. Elizabeth's actions had touched a raw nerve, and he did not want to be reminded of how devoted he and Amelia had been to the church and God.

"I am sorry," Elizabeth's tears began once again and she wiped them away and looked down, but more took their place, and he felt like a heel. These were not like the earlier ones that she had shed when she was lost in her worship of God. These were the tears of a hurting woman.

"Miss Elizabeth, we need to go, because it will be dark soon and it is not safe to be out here in the dark."

"Yes, yes of course," she sniffed.

He sighed inwardly, clicked, and got Misty going.

CHAPTER FOUR

MISSOULA, MONTANA
SPRING, 1874

Elizabeth allowed William to lift her off the horse, and when he set her down she looked around her in dismay. This was primitive land. It was dusk and through the dim light she could make out the log cabin that was to be her home until the day she died. She heard a cow lowing in the distance and the evening birds were chirping greetings to each other.

"Welcome to your new home, Miss Elizabeth," William said. She was glad of the fading light, so that he could not see the expression on her face. She knew that the west was not as advanced as Boston, but even this was too primitive for her. She expected Virginia to begin whining, but when she looked around the young girl was nowhere to be seen.

"Miss Virginia has led the horse to the back of the house, or actually Spitfire led herself there," William had answered her unspoken question.

"Oh!"

"Well, the girls are inside waiting, no doubt." The front door opened and two girls ran down the two steps and flung themselves at William. "Or not," he muttered before lifting each of them and swinging them high.

That he loved his daughters was obvious to Elizabeth at that point, and she felt a little bit calm. A man who loved his children and expressed it without reservation could not be that bad. She was still remembering the tone of voice he had used a little while ago. He did not understand what she was feeling, and she had felt as though it was a mistake for her to have come. But now she 'schooled' her expression and waited to meet her future daughters.

The two girls, after greeting their father stood silently beside him, clutching at his overalls, and looked at Elizabeth. She could not read their expressions very well in the poor light.

"Girls, this is Miss Elizabeth, soon to be your new mama," he told them, gently prodding them so they could go forward and greet Elizabeth. "Take her to the house. I need to put the horses away." He took the portmanteau and violin down and carried them to the porch as the six female eyes followed his every move. "I will carry those through when I am done with the animals."

They watched him lead Black Thunder and Misty to the back of the house and then Elizabeth looked at the girls, who were still a few feet away from her.

"My name is Elizabeth Anne Lowell, as your papa has told

you." She looked at Mary. "You must be Mary, and you must be Abigail." She broke the silence at last. She took a small step in their direction in order not to scare them off. The girls looked a bit wary of her. She smiled and her dimples showed.

"You have a pretty home. I can't wait for you to show it to me tomorrow, when there is light." She took another step forward. The girls did not move, but neither did they run away, and she took this as a good sign.

"Is Misty your horse?" She looked from one to the other and Mary shook her head.

"Misty is nobody's horse," Abigail answered. "She is so old that no one wants her anymore." There was a wistful tone in the girl's voice.

"Oh, but I love her," Elizabeth cried out. "She was so good to me, and did not throw me at all." The two girls looked at each other and then giggled.

"Misty does not throw people," Mary giggled. "Aunt Kate calls her a lump of a lazy horse."

"But I did not know that. Do you want to know something?" Elizabeth asked no one in particular, and both girls nodded simultaneously. "I was so afraid of horses because, you see, I had never ridden on one before today."

The girls' eyes opened wide. They could not imagine that anyone had never ridden a horse in their lives before.

"Really?" Mary drew closer and unconsciously slipped her hand into Elizabeth's. Abigail hesitated only for a moment, and then imitated her sister's actions.

"Yes, really. You see in Boston there are many horses, but they only pull carriages and coaches. I have ridden in coaches and carriages, but never on a horse."

Abigail skipped lightly, her hand in Elizabeth's. "It is not hard to learn."

"Yes, I know that, thanks to Misty." Elizabeth smiled. "Shall we go in and see what needs to be done?"

Because it was late, the family had a simple meal of rough whole wheat bread and milk. The three watched as Elizabeth and Virginia thoroughly washed their hands before sitting down for the meal. They had cleaned their hands, but not as thoroughly as they saw the visitors do it. And then, when they would have reached for their food, Elizabeth's words caused them to halt.

"Shall we pray?" She looked around the crude table that was set in the kitchen. It was a big round table that was made for six people. Mary was on her left and Virginia on her right. Next to Virginia was Abigail, and William sat next to his youngest daughter. This left an empty seat between William and Mary.

Elizabeth had watched curiously as Mary reached into the cabinet and removed a coffee mug. She placed it next to her own mug, and Elizabeth raised her eyes questioningly to William. In the flickering candle light she saw a silent plea in his eyes and so made no mention of the mug, especially when after their simple supper, Mary put it back in the cabinet unused. She would ask William about all that later.

Right now she was tired and wished she could take a long bath to wash away three weeks of travel fatigue, but looking around her she did not see the possibilities of that happening, at least not tonight.

"Mary will show you where you will sleep." William stood up. "I have to secure the animals for the night." He went out the back door and the four ladies were left alone. Virginia was dropping. She looked exhausted, and Elizabeth's heart welled with compassion for her little sister.

"Come girls. Let us all go to bed now." The young girls stood up, as did Virginia. "Mary, show us the way."

Mary picked up one candle and led the group down a short corridor and opened the door at the furthest end. Elizabeth brought up the rear, carrying another candle. There were two other doors that they passed but these were closed. Elizabeth was too tired to inquire what lay beyond those closed doors. Tomorrow would reveal the mysteries of this house. There were two beds in the room, obviously the girls' beds.

Mary moved closer to Elizabeth. "Will you sleep with me?"

"Sure." Elizabeth smiled at the child. "Let us get you ready for bed." She expected that the girls would find night clothes, but was surprised when they jumped into bed in the clothes they had on, which they had obviously spent the day in. She shook her head. There would be time to make changes later. For now, the beds beckoned.

Virginia climbed into bed after Abigail and was immediately fast asleep. The two girls followed suit, and Elizabeth blew the candle out and sat in the darkness. She had not heard William coming in and so knew that he probably was still taking care of the animals.

"Lord, what do you have in store for us in this land?" She whispered the prayer. "I have held on to my faith in You to lead us here, and because we have arrived it means You have a bigger plan for our lives in this land. Mr. William seems like a fine man, and his children are absolute darlings. This is a family that we need, and also needs us. Guide my every step as I live in this home, and help me make good decisions concerning the welfare of Abigail, Mary, and also Virginia. And I want to once again express my gratitude to you, Lord, for making William send for us, and for getting us out of Boston before Virginia lost her virtue and soul in that place. And as we sleep tonight, watch over all of us, including

Misty, Black Thunder, Spitfire, and all the other animals. In Jesus' name, amen."

William crept back into the house when he was sure everyone was asleep. He did not want to meet with Elizabeth, not tonight. He locked the doors securely and then entered his bedroom. In the candlelight he looked at his unmade bed and sighed. He had to shake it out before he got in because he did not want any 'surprise' creatures sharing the bed with him.

He took off his boots tiredly, and his overalls and shirt followed suit. He left his drawstring on, and after giving his bedding a thorough shaking, he made up the bed roughly and got in. He lay on his back and put his hands at the back of his head.

"Amelia, I miss you," he murmured. He wondered what Elizabeth thought of his house and children. She had come in when it was dark, and in the candlelight she could not have seen how scruffy everything was. She would see the true state of affairs in the morning.

William twisted his lips. Why should he care what she thought? She was to be his wife in name only. Nothing else mattered. But he felt a bit of discomfiture. He had met the woman only today, and already she was getting under his skin.

At the supper table she had made it feel as though they were a family, and he did not want to feel that way with any other woman except Amelia. He remembered meal times with his dead wife and his eyes watered. Amelia had been so full of life and hope, and in an instant, that life had been snuffed out of her and just like that, she was gone forever. Now Elizabeth was here to take her place. Well, she could be mother to his children and that was that. So far she did not look like she expected much else from him, but he would be very cautious. No need stirring up feelings in the woman which he could not satisfy.

He decided that he would keep his distance, and was glad that summer was almost here. He could disappear into the mountains with Sure Foot to capture more horses. Staying around the homestead might make him begin to have feelings for Elizabeth, who he admitted, reluctantly, was a very beautiful woman. He would never betray his first love.

"Amelia, I will never love another, and betray you."

~~~ *** ~~~

The next morning Elizabeth woke up early and went outside to look for the outhouse. She ran back screaming when she found a snake coiled near the building, which was a distance away from the house. William, who was milking the cows, rushed out of the barn to see what was going on.

"A sn—, sn—ake!" She pointed at the outhouse, and William went to see which kind of snake it was. He was just in time to see the green reptile slithering away into the tall grass, glad it was a harmless one. Just a grass snake which was more frightened of people. But he did not tell that to his betrothed, who was shaking like a leaf.

Elizabeth was so terrified. Would she survive in this place? She wondered. "God, help me, please," she begged silently.

"The snake has gone and I have checked inside. There are no other unwanted visitors, so you can go ahead and use the outhouse."

"Th—, thank you," she stammered and walked cautiously to the outhouse.

The interior of the house was another matter altogether. The house had been well built with sturdy logs and the cracks filled with sod. The roof was also made of sod and logs and beams, and because it was almost summer, the sod had started coming lose and particles of it were everywhere. This was a disaster, according to Elizabeth. Would she ever get the place sorted out? The three girls were still asleep, and she did not know where to start. She walked through the house. It was a large house and the space made her smile in the midst of her dismay. This was a house that had been built with a large family in mind, and she could feel the love emitting from the walls, but it was tinged with sadness. The floor was made of small wooden tiles, and Elizabeth was amazed at the beauty in the early morning. It reminded her of their house in

Boston and deep sadness filled her heart, but she pushed the thoughts away and continued with her tour of the house.

Somehow, without being told, she knew that William had built this house for his first wife, and he had done it with a lot of love. Given time and with a lot of work, she could restore it to what she imagined it to have been when her predecessor was alive.

She started with the large sitting room, which extended from the kitchen. It was a rectangular room and the porch outside went the length of it. On the outer wall there was a fireplace, which no doubt kept the whole house warm during winter. She had heard that winters in the Rockies could be very cold. There was a mantle above the fireplace and there were three large photos on it. She was curious to see what William's first wife had looked like. There were four rough, straight-back seats and a small table, the sum of all the furniture in the sitting room. She picked up the first dust-covered photo which had a wooden back holding it. She immediately recognized William as the man in the photo. He was standing over a woman who was seated with a baby on her lap and another sitting at her feet. The woman was so beautiful.

"That is Amelia." Elizabeth turned around quickly. She had not heard William come in. "My wife."

Elizabeth silently nodded. The man was still in love with his wife and she felt a slight pang, but dismissed it. She was here to marry the man for the shelter and protection he could provide, and she had better remember that. She lost interest in looking at the photos and looked around the room.

"You have a beautiful house," she said.

"Why do I sense as though there is a 'but' in there somewhere?" William entered further into the room.

Elizabeth sighed. "There is dust everywhere," she waved her hands helplessly. "How will it ever get clean?"

"Now that summer is here I will make some repairs to the roof before I leave for the mountains," he said in his deep voice. "I already milked and if you do not mind, I would like to show you the rest of the house before breakfast."

"I would like that very much," she said.

"Come with me, please." He led the way out of the sitting room and to the corridor. "This is my bedroom," he pointed at one of the doors that she had seen yesterday. "And this one is Amelia's bedroom," he pointed at the second closed door, and Elizabeth's eyebrows went up. As far as she knew married people were supposed to share a bedroom. William sensed her silent question. "Amelia used to say that I toss and turn around a lot, and so she could not get enough sleep."

"Oh!"

"Then there is the room that you and the girls slept in." He led the way back to the kitchen. He opened a door which she had not noticed the night before. She saw sacks of flour and tins whose contents she would explore later. "This is the pantry. During winter, we can store fresh vegetables and meat and milk in here, and it does not go bad for three days or so. But during spring and summer, we only store dry flour and cereals." He closed the door. "And this is the kitchen." He waved his right hand. "I will have to teach you how to use the cooking range. It was Amelia's pride and joy. She could cook anything on this thing." He opened the outer door and stepped out into the yard, which Elizabeth had a chance to see properly now that it was lighter.

"Come this way, and I will show you the barn. Actually, it is a stable on one side and a barn on the other." They walked in silence and she drew her shawl closer to her. It was a bit chilly. They entered a large room and Elizabeth smiled when she saw Misty, who made a sound as if recognizing her.

"Oh Misty, good morning," she went and patted her gently.

"Misty remembers you," William said with a smile. "And you remember Spitfire and Black Thunder." There were three other horses. "This is Morning Dew, and she belongs to Abigail. Moon Flower belongs to Mary, and Primrose here is Amelia's horse."

"I thought you said you run a horse ranch?" She looked around to see if there were more horses in the large stable.

"I rear mustangs, which are bought by miners and some soldiers, as well as the stagecoach owners. They are feral animals, and prefer the wild rather than being kept in a stable."

"So, where are they?"

"Out in the mountains."

"Who looks after them while they are there?"

"They are free-spirited creatures, and my friend Sure Foot watches over them for me."

"Sure Foot?"

"Yes. He is a Nez Perce Indian chief."

"Okay."

He led her past the stable and into the barn. "This is where I keep the other animals. We have four cows. Two are pregnant and two have calves, and so we have a lot of milk. Amelia used to make butter, and would sell it in Hellgate," he said. "We also have some chickens. They were Amelia's, and when she was still here she had about fifty of them. Now we have only a handful, so we do not get as many eggs as before." He looked around. "I let the goats out earlier, because they are such impatient creatures, unlike the cows."

"How many are there?"

"Just six. Abigail and Mary will help you with the milking and the animals when I am gone. They know what to do, because I taught them."

"Where does the water come from? The water we use in the house?"

"There is a stream just a short distance away, and that is the water that we use to drink. And there is also a well." He led her to the well. It was nicely covered, no doubt to safeguard the children and animals.

"When I am not here, do not go down to the stream. I will always make sure that you have enough water to drink before I leave. Use the well water for washing and other things, and spare the one from the stream for drinking."

"Okay, Mr. William."

William pointed at a large flat rock beside the barn. "This is a good place to hang the beddings, whenever you need to. The rock retains heat, and if there are any insects in the clothes, the heat soon kills them. Beyond that is a small garden that Amelia kept for spices and herbs. No one has tilled it since she died."

Once breakfast was over, William took himself out of the house and disappeared on horseback. Elizabeth looked at the three girls. She had an old scarf over her head to hold her unruly curls. Her hair was growing and she would have to trim it sometime.

"We have a lot of work to do, ladies. First, we have to clean our bedroom thoroughly."

Over the first few days the four ladies got down to cleaning the house thoroughly and slowly, and slowly it was beginning to take its shape and recover its former glory. Though Virginia assisted with the household chores, she grumbled about the hard work most of the time, and many times Elizabeth let her play truant. Better to do the work alone than have a whining person distressing her.

William had repaired the roof, so no more dust found its way into the house. They cleaned and dusted, and one of the things that really delighted Elizabeth was the discovery of an old metal tub in the barn. William had previously used it for watering the animals, but when Mary told Elizabeth that it had been her mother's bathing tub, that decided it for her.

She had brought some sweet smelling bathing soap from Boston, and though she knew she would have to use it sparingly, nevertheless she decided that on Saturdays the girls would bathe with it as a treat in readiness for Sunday. The rest of the days they could use the crude lard soap that had a strong, distasteful smell.

On their first Saturday, Elizabeth made sure they all finished their chores early enough. Of William, there was no sign. She had actually not seen him for two days, but she knew that if he was to leave for the mountains, he would inform her.

"Girls, we have to prepare for church tomorrow."

"Church?" Mary and Amelia chorused, looking at each other.

"Why are you saying it like that?" she asked the girls.

Mary twisted her lips. "We do not go to church, Miss Elizabeth."

"Why not?" She was so shocked. She knew that the children did not know their prayers, and had thought that probably the church they attended did not have Sunday school. She had decided that when they went to church, she would speak to the pastor and see if she could offer her services as a Sunday school teacher. But now to hear that they did not go to church almost floored her. She remembered that when she had seen William's advert, he had indicated that he was a Christian.

"And your father? Does he go to church?" The two girls shook their heads, and Elizabeth tightened her lips. She would talk to William when he got back, but he did not turn up, not even by the time they were leaving for the church.

Elizabeth enjoyed the service very much. She met Pastor Thomas and his wife Salome, and a few other families. The children were also happy to go to church, especially because they had new dresses to wear. Elizabeth had tucked the girls into two of Virginia's old dresses, and though they were long they fit the girls very well. She had used her brush on Mary's hair each night, and the girl's hair now sparkled. She shook her head at Abigail's mop.

After a lunch of roast potatoes and beans, washed down with a cup of milk, the four sat on the porch and Elizabeth brought out her violin. She began to play and Virginia started by singing:

"Oh Lord, my God, how great Thou art." The young girls stared at Virginia in awe. She had an angelic voice, and because she loved to sing it came from the heart. They sang fun songs which Elizabeth and Virginia taught them, accompanied by Elizabeth on the violin, and the four of them had a good laugh. And that was how William found them.

On his way back from the lower range he had heard the sweet violin sound and stood still. His betrothed was good, and the music brought nostalgia and a restlessness which he could not explain. Immediately, when Elizabeth saw him, she stopped playing and put her violin away.

"I hope I did not interrupt your playing, Miss Elizabeth," he said.

"No." She stood up. "It is almost time for me to begin preparing the evening meal."

"Can we help, Miss Elizabeth?" Mary stood up.

"Well, you have all been very good this week, so I am giving you today off. Take Virginia and go and pick some flowers for the table."

"Yay!" the girls cheered, and ran down the porch.

William looked at Elizabeth and she looked right back at him. The look in her eye told him she wanted to talk, and it was a serious matter indeed. He had seen that look in Amelia's eyes many times. Without being told, he followed Elizabeth into the kitchen. Her back was straight and he knew she was angry.

"Unless you tell me what I have done to offend you, then I cannot beg your forgiveness." He took off his hat and sat down at the table.

"Why did you lie to me?"

He frowned. "When did I lie to you?"

"Your advert said you were a Christian man, and yet I do not see you praying, you did not attend church today, and I have seen your smoking pipe."

He held his head in his hands and then let out a long breath. "Truthfully, it is Mary who sent in that advert. And I stopped smoking the pipe ten years ago when Amelia and I got married. It is just a reminder of the old days."

"Oh, so you are telling me that you did not want a wife, and it was your young twelve-year-old daughter that placed the advert for you?"

"Yes."

"I don't believe you." She held her waist. "Your daughters can barely read, and I am made to understand that they do not go to school. And secondly, they do not go to church, and neither do you."

"I guess everyone has their preferences."

"Is that right?" She moved to where he was seated and stood before him. "Well, I will tell you one thing. You brought me here under false pretenses, and so I am a wronged party."

"What do you mean?"

"When I agreed to come west and you sent me the money to come and be wed to you, we entered into some sort of contract. But this is no longer a valid contract, because one party lied to the other, and so it cannot hold up in a court of law."

"Court of law? Woman, what are you going on about?"

"The law clearly stipulates that if one of us breaks the contract that we entered into, then the guilty party is liable to pay damages to the aggrieved party. I am aggrieved, and I can easily take this matter to the nearest judge, to see that justice is done for me."

"Judge? What is going on?"

"The advert that you placed in the paper, of which I have a copy and will produce it as evidence if need be, clearly states that you are a Christian man. That is the reason I entered into correspondence with you, and agreed to come out here and be your wife. Now I get here and realize that you are a behaving like a pagan, and brought me here under false pretenses. That is a serious misdeed on your part, and for which I ought to seek redress."

William stared open-mouthed at his betrothed. But she was not done with him yet.

"You knew about my faith, and I am not ashamed of the Cross of Christ, which you clearly are. Amos in the Bible says, 'Two cannot walk together unless they be agreed.'" She twisted her lips. "We are clearly not going to be agreed on the matter of our faith, and in which case I absolve you of your part in the contract, and I will stay here long enough to earn enough money for transport to take Virginia and me back to Boston, and we will be gone. I cannot marry someone who does not share my faith, because I do not intend to have a house full of strife as we pull in different directions. So, there is no marriage that is going to happen between you and me, and since you are the one more at fault here, I beg that you allow us to stay here a few days and work for you, and you will then pay our fare back to Boston." And with that said she picked up a pail and left the kitchen, clearly intending to go and get some water.

William was stunned for a while. He ought to have known that this problem would come up, especially since the first day when he had looked at Elizabeth's face and seen the glow as she worshipped the Lord upon sighting the Rocky Mountains. In the few days that they had been here, he had realized that his soon-to-be wife was very devoted to her faith, and many times he found her seated at the table with a bowed head, deep in prayer.

Elizabeth prepared dinner and after dinner she cleaned the dishes as the girls sang songs in the sitting room.

"Will you play the violin for us again?" Mary begged, and Elizabeth smiled.

"Of course, little girl. Remember, we have started having our devotions and music from the heart, which is pleasant to the Lord."

William did not take part in the devotions but sat on the porch. When he was sure that they had finished, he stepped into the sitting room.

"Miss Elizabeth, may I speak with you?"

Elizabeth motioned for Virginia to take the girls to bed, and she put her violin away and stepped onto the porch.

"Please sit," he pointed at one of the seats. There were three on the porch, one that could sit two people and the others made for only one person. She sat on one single seat and waited, her hands on her lap.

"When Amelia was alive, we used to go to church every

Sunday, and we took part in all the activities that went on there. I trusted in the God that you profess, but He let me down."

"How?" Elizabeth asked, though she already knew the answer.

"Amelia was only twenty-eight, and we had a lot of plans and dreams for our family, and I loved her so much. Why did God have to take her away from us? Is that love?" He was almost shouting.

"Do not raise your voice at me," Elizabeth said in a firm voice. "Lower your voice, because the children are not yet asleep."

"I am sorry," he said. "If it is important to you that I appear in church every Sunday when

I am here, then that is alright. Standing in a building should do no harm, I guess. But do not expect me to profess what I do not feel. I would rather be called an unbeliever than a hypocrite, Miss Elizabeth." Elizabeth was silent for a while. "It is also alright for the children to go to school and Sunday school, if that will make you happy, Miss Elizabeth."

Elizabeth sighed. He just did not get it, but this was not the time to argue.

"Miss Elizabeth?"

"Yes, Mr. William?"

"Will you reconsider your decision about returning to Boston? I, er, the children need you. I have seen how good they are looking, and in just the short span of a week. Please, for their sake, please agree to stay and be their mother. And I promise that I will go to church with you every Sunday."

Elizabeth looked up. "I will put that to the test. For the next four Sundays, you will accompany us to church, and the fifth Saturday from now, we will be wed, that is, if you keep your end of the bargain."

"I am a man of my word, Miss Elizabeth. And I give you my solemn promise."

"What about when you go out with the horses?"

"I will be sure to return every Saturday."

And William kept his word and accompanied his family to church for the next four Sundays, much to Pastor Thomas' joy. The elderly clergyman kept laughing and rubbing his balding head. His black eyes sparkled merrily.

"Glory to God, glory to God," he kept repeating, beaming at his wife and William's family.

Even though William sat at the back and refused to join them in the family pew, and he would not open his mouth to sing any of the hymns, to Elizabeth it was still a small victory. She had hoped that he would at least show some interest, but she comforted herself with the knowledge that he at least went to church.

They had a small wedding, given that both of them had agreed that it was to be in name only.

"Hypocrisy is a vice I have no wish of indulging in," Elizabeth said. "No need for people to come here and believe that we are going to have happy wedded bliss, and yet this is a business arrangement."

"I agree with you, Miss Elizabeth."

And so it was that only Salome and Kate were witnesses during the wedding, as well as the three younger girls, and one wrangler who had shown up asking for work, and William had put him to work cleaning the barn. When he left for the mountains he would be taking Theodore with him because he did not trust a stranger with his family.

After the wedding, as the small group enjoyed the cake and food that Salome and Kate had prepared back at the house, Elizabeth motioned to William, and he followed her to the porch.

"And I hope you are not going to take it into your mind to begin absconding from church just because I wear your ring now," she challenged. "In any case, as a business arrangement we are not going to consummate this marriage, and that will be my defense should you decide to renege this contract."

"No, of course not. I told you my word is my bond, and it is my purpose to make sure that you are happy. So, Miss Elizabeth, rest easy. I will be here every Saturday in time to accompany all of you to church on Sundays."

"Thank you," she held out her hand and he looked at it in surprise. "Let us shake hands, as honorable people do when entering into an agreement."

CHAPTER FIVE

Elizabeth was baking, and had just removed the first batch of scones from the oven when the back door opened and Abigail practically shot into the kitchen, dropped her school bag and burst into tears.

"What is wrong?" Elizabeth pulled the sobbing girl into her arms and held her close.

"They said I am an idiot," Abigail wailed. "I will never go back to that school again!"

"Hush, little one." Elizabeth led her to the table and made her sit down. She poured her a glass of milk and put a hot scone on a saucer and gave it to the girl. She ignored the fact that the girl had not washed her hands. This was not the time for hygiene lessons, when clearly the child was distraught. But to her surprise, Abigail stood up and walked to the stone sink and washed her hands thoroughly, as Elizabeth had taught her over the days.

"What happened in school, Abigail?" Elizabeth asked when the girl had devoured her scone and downed her milk.

"The other girls are always teasing me about my short hair, and they say that I look like a boy. They also keep saying that I am dumb and I am an idiot, because I cannot read and I do not know how to write."

"Oh child," Elizabeth pulled her off her chair and onto her lap. "You are not dumb and you are not an idiot, okay? And you are a very intelligent and beautiful girl."

"But they are right! I can't read or write." She started crying again. "I will never go back to school again. I will stay with Misty, Moon Flower, Morning Dew and Primrose. They never laugh at me or mock me."

"Then I will teach you to read." Elizabeth held the child close. "Those children who say you are an idiot are misguided, because they do not know your strengths and capabilities, Abigail. If you refuse to go back, then you are letting them win, and you will always think that you were not good enough to be in school with them, and they will always call you names because you did not prove them otherwise. Do you understand what I am saying, Abby?" The child nodded. "This is what I will do. Every day when you return from school, I will help you with your homework, and if you have any questions or anything that you do not understand, do not be afraid to ask me, okay?"

"Yes, Mama."

Elizabeth held the child at arm's length. "What did you say?" she asked in a whisper. "What did you call me?"

"Mama?" Abigail smiled through her tears, and Elizabeth's eyes welled up with tears.

"Oh, my baby," she whispered huskily, hugging the child close.

Two days later Mary would not get out of bed, and Elizabeth was concerned when Virginia came and told her that the child had burrowed under the beddings and would not talk to her.

"Mary, honey?" Elizabeth sat on the bed that she still shared with the child. She touched the back of Mary's head. "What is wrong?"

"My stomach hurts," the muffled response came from under the pillow.

"When did it start?"

"Last night." Elizabeth nodded. The child had been very restless and her tossing and turning had caused Elizabeth to have very little sleep.

"What else are you feeling?" There was silence for a while, and then Elizabeth heard soft sobs.

"What is it, child?"

"I, I, I," she could not speak.

"You did what, Mary?"

"I wet the bed. I am sorry."

Elizabeth smiled. Without letting the child know what she was doing, she gently lifted the bedding in such a way that Mary did not realize it. When she saw what she was looking for, she nodded.

"Okay, stay here. I am coming back, okay?"

"Yes."

Elizabeth went to the yard and lifted the large tub, and carried it to the bedroom. She then went and heated some water, all the while checking on the child, who was still in bed. When the bathwater was ready, she gently coaxed the child to rise up.

"You have not wet the bed, Mary," she said gently.

"But I have!" Mary would not even look down. She held the beddings to her chest.

"No, child," Elizabeth shook her head. "What is happening is very normal for every girl and every woman." She checked to see if the child was listening. She was. "Your period has started."

"Period?"

"Yes, Mary. That is when a young girl transitions, or becomes a woman. Now you are becoming a young woman. You are not a child anymore."

"Why?"

"Because that is how God created women to be. When you

become a woman, now your body is preparing itself for one day when you will become a mother. Do you understand what I am saying?"

"I think so, but will I be wetting my bed every day?"

"It is not pee, Mary. That is blood."

"Blood?" Mary almost screamed and quickly looked at herself and saw the evidence of what Elizabeth was explaining. "Will I die?"

"No child, that is very normal. And it will happen for three to four days, and then stop until the next month. Nothing to worry about. That is the mark of a lady, and you should be very proud of yourself, that you are a normal and healthy woman."

That night Mary did not sleep because of the menstrual cramps, and Elizabeth had to keep rubbing her back, and at one point she got up and went to the kitchen, where the embers were still glowing in the wood stove, and she boiled some water and crushed a ginger root and added it to the boiling water, and took it to the child.

"Drink this. It will make you feel better." She held out the mug of ginger concoction and watched as Mary drank it all. A little while later the girl settled down and was soon asleep. But Elizabeth's sleep had been disturbed and she tightened her lips. She was going to make drastic changes to this household. After all, she was now the woman of the house.

She waited for the children to go to school before she undertook the task that she knew would probably create some tension when William came back. Virginia, who had taken to the horses, was in the back yard with Spitfire and she was practicing how to get on and off the horse in the shortest time possible.

Elizabeth walked to the room that William had told her had been Amelia's, and she turned the door knob. It opened and she stood at the door, letting her eyes adjust to the darkness within. It was also a large room and she noticed it had two beds in it, but one was larger. She walked to the window and drew back the thick curtains and opened the window.

Her mouth fell open when she saw the room under proper lighting. This looked like a shrine. The layers of dust that had accumulated made her realize that probably no one had entered this room since Amelia died.

"What a waste," she thought to herself. There were two trunks in the room, and when she opened them she found rows and rows of soft dresses and linens, petticoats, chemises, bonnets. They were all very pretty, and some were almost new. There was a small table on which were a number of Amelia's personal effects, also quite dusty. She shook her head.

"What are you doing?"

She started when she heard Virginia's voice. "Oh Virginia, you startled me."

"What are you doing in here?"

"I am making a room for myself, is what I am doing."

"Did you ask William for permission?"

"I do not need to. I am the new mistress of this house, and so I have a right to put my house in order. This here is a wasted room, and yet we four are squeezed in that one room. And the girls are growing bigger, so it is time they stopped sharing a bed."

"That is true, but shouldn't you wait for William to give you permission first?"

"He will not do that," Elizabeth indicated with her hand. "This is a shrine to his dead wife, and he is not going to let go unless I change things. But, do not worry. I am not throwing anything out. I will simply dust them and move them to his room, which is large enough to contain these trunks and other stuff that belonged to his dead wife. He can build her a shrine there, and gaze at it whenever he wants to. But I am tired of not getting enough sleep, and yet I have to do so much work during the day. If this will be the reason for him to ask me for a divorce, then let him."

Virginia just shook her head and went to sit on the porch. She looked into the distance and sighed. This place was stifling her and she wished she could leave, but where would she go? If she did not have Spitfire she would have gone mad by now. Having the horse enabled her to take long rides in the mountains and she enjoyed her secret trips, even though she knew William would probably forbid her if he found out. Then she smiled, an idea forming in her mind.

She would go to Hellgate, but without letting Elizabeth know what she was doing. With that thought, she hurried to change into a riding skirt, and shouting to Elizabeth that she was taking Spitfire for a ride. She then left.

Meanwhile, Elizabeth dusted the two trunks and dragged them to William's room. While he was away, she had aired the room and his mattress and washed the sheets and quilt. She had cleaned the room and washed his dirty clothes and neatly folded them into his trunk. She knew that he had not given her permission to invade his privacy, but neither had he forbidden her to enter his domain.

"Besides, it is a wife's duty to ensure that her husband is clean, and that his room is also clean," she thought. Now she lifted the trunks and placed them one on top of the other. Everything that had belonged to Amelia she neatly placed in William's room, and then made up the two beds in the bedroom. She would bring Mary to sleep in this room with her, and Virginia and Abigail could share the other bedroom.

CHAPTER SIX

William was livid when he returned and found that Amelia's room had been tampered with. He had wondered why Elizabeth seemed nervous immediately as he had arrived, but it was only until he went to his bedroom and saw Amelia's things that he realized what she had done.

"This woman has crossed the line," he silently fumed. "Who does she think she is?"

Supper was a strained affair, and when it was over Virginia motioned for the two girls to follow her to their room, leaving Elizabeth and William in the kitchen. From the look of things, they would not be having their evening devotions.

"Why did you enter Amelia's room and mess with her things?"

"First of all, I did not mess with anything," Elizabeth said. "And secondly, if you have not noticed, I am now the woman of the house."

"And what is that supposed to mean?"

"It means that I deserve some respect as your wife, Mr. William. Mary is a growing child, and it is not fair for me to squeeze with her on her bed, and the same goes for Abigail. And yet, there is a large room with two beds that is lying unused in this house."

"That is my wife's room."

"No," Elizabeth shook her head. "That is not a room. It is a shrine."

"How dare you say that?"

"I dare, because it is true. Mr. William, those trunks contain beautiful clothes that I can adjust to fit Mary and Abigail, and yet you have kept them to be feasted on by moths."

"Who gave you permission to touch Amelia's things?"

"Amelia is dead," Elizabeth hissed. She did not want the children to hear them arguing. "I respect and honor her memory, but she is dead, and your children are alive, as I am. I cannot continue to spend sleepless nights, as your daughter tosses in bed because it is too small for the two of us. If you do not want me to use that room then so be it, I can make my bed here in the kitchen, and sleep here."

William stood up. "You should not have touched Amelia's things," he said and left the room. She heard him enter his room and a short while later heard him dragging something, and she realized he was taking the trunks back to Amelia's room. She tightened her lips. So it was like that. Well, he was about to find out what she was made of.

For two days the house was tense and the usual laughter was missing. Even the evening devotions were strained, and Elizabeth only played sad songs on the violin. Elizabeth's eyes were swollen from so much crying, and also she had been sleeping in the kitchen on the floor, and her back was aching. But she would not complain.

Mary followed her father to the stables on the third day. She found him feeding the horses.

"It is only a room," the quiet child said, and William looked at her in surprise.

"What, Mary?"

"I said it is only a room. Mama is dead and is not coming back, Papa. Miss Elizabeth is a good person, and she deserves to have her own room. You don't have to be mad."

William put down the shovel and looked at his daughter. "I am not mad because of the room. I am mad because she did not ask me before she touched your mother's things."

"If she had asked you to move mama's things, would you have agreed, Pa?" William thought for a while and then shook his head.

"You know, Pa, while you were gone, I was so sick, and Miss

Elizabeth did not get any sleep at all. She looked after me all the time, and even now she is so tired." The child shook her head. "I don't think it is fair that you refuse to let her sleep in that room which is empty, Pa, and now she is sleeping in the kitchen, and won't come to our room."

"What?" William was shocked at this new information.

"Miss Elizabeth is a good woman, Pa. She is a good mama to us. Do you know that Abigail is now learning how to read and write, and she likes going to school? And she has taught me how to do so many things, Pa. We love going to church, because we are learning new songs and stories, Papa." The child sighed. "Missing Mama does not hurt so much, because Miss Elizabeth loves us. Why can't you be kind to her, even a little?" Mary turned and left her father deep in thought.

He finished feeding the animals and then went to the house. Elizabeth was asleep at the kitchen table and he stood watching her for a while. He saw the lines of fatigue on her face and the dried tears. When he looked at her hands, he almost cried. They were blistered and some of the blisters had burst open, leaving the skin red and raw, and they looked painful. But he had not heard her complain about anything. He also noticed how her clothes hung on her. She had lost weight, but she bore it all with strength and in silence. He felt really low.

This was a delicate woman who ought to have had servants and lived the life of comfort that she had been accustomed to. Instead, she had chosen to come to this ranch and be his wife. She worked hard without complaining and she deserved a good place to sleep. And he was being selfish by denying her a good place to rest. And all because it was his dead wife's bedroom. He went to Amelia's room and looked around. He shifted the trunks back to his bedroom. He remembered that Elizabeth had told him there were good clothes that she could adjust to fit the young girls. He would look at them later.

Right now he had a tired wife to care for. He was glad he had not touched the beds and had left them as Elizabeth had made them. He pulled down the covers of the larger bed and went to the kitchen.

Elizabeth did not stir when he carried her to the bedroom and placed her on the bed. That was when he realized just how tired she must have been. And she was not as heavy as he had expected her to be. He tucked her in and kissed her forehead, surprising even himself, and then he hurriedly left the room, closing the door.

~~~ *** ~~~

Virginia watched as Abigail roped Morning Dew and copied her. The three girls were getting ready to ride. William allowed them to exercise the horses around the homestead as long as they did not venture out of sight.

"Mary, is Papa still mad at Mama?" Abigail asked, her voice trembling.

"I don't know," Mary sighed. "I love Mama so much. I wish Pa wouldn't be mad at her. I don't want her to leave."

"Leave?" Abigail raised stricken eyes to her sister and she burst into tears. "I don't want Mama to leave us again." Mary also started crying.

Virginia dropped the rope and gathered the girls to her. "Hush, girls," she soothed, leading them to the large flat rock on which they aired any items that needed airing. She sat down with either girl on her side.

"Stop crying. Lizzie is not leaving, and neither am I."

"But if Pa is mad at her, she might want to leave us and go back to Boston," Mary said in a teary voice.

"Lizzie loves the two of you so much. She would never leave you, no matter what. She is now your mother and mamas do not leave their children."

"But our first mama left us," Abigail said in a small voice.

"That is true, but she left because she went to heaven, to be with Jesus. Remember, we have been learning that at church." The girls nodded. "Lizzie is now your mama. And your pa is allowed to be mad at her because they are married. Pas and Mas are usually mad at each other, but then, because they love each other, they soon make up and are happy again, together."

"Ginnie?"

"Yes, Mary?"

"Where is your ma?"

"She is in heaven."

"And your pa?"

"In heaven, with Ma."

"Did they die together?"

"No, Mary." Virginia shook her head. "Ma died when I was young, and Lizzie looked after me. She is very kind and caring, and just like my ma." She thought for a while. "I cannot even remember what Mama looked like. Lizzie is the one who has been looking after me all this time."

"She is very nice, and I love her," Abigail said.

"I also love her," Mary agreed. "And from today, I will never call her Miss Elizabeth again. I will call her Mama."

"Yes, even me."

Virginia smiled, as did William who was in the stables and had heard the girls' conversation.

When Elizabeth woke up it was dark, and there was a lit candle on the small table in the room. She sat up and frowned, looking around her. She did not remember coming to bed, and this certainly was not Mary's bed. She realized that she was in Amelia's room, and for a moment sat in deep thought. Had she been sleepwalking and ended up in this room because her mind had been set on using it? But if she had sleepwalked, shouldn't she be on top of the covers? She was tucked in nicely, as though someone had put her to bed, and she wondered.

She slowly got out of bed and stretched. She felt very refreshed, and picking up the candle she went to the kitchen where she found William seated at the table with the two young girls. Virginia was at the stove stirring something.

"Mama," Abigail pushed back her chair and ran to Elizabeth. "Are you alright? Pa told us you were not feeling well, and we should not disturb you."

Mary also came and hugged Elizabeth. "Yes Ma, we were worried about you."

"No need to be." Elizabeth refused to look at William, afraid that she would see the anger in his eyes. "I was just a little tired."

"Girls, let your ma at least rest before you bombard her with your stuff," she heard William say, and she looked at him quickly. There was a strange expression on his face. He stood up and pulled out a chair for Elizabeth.

"Ma?"

"Yes, Abby?"

"Ginnie is making us fish stew."

"Really? Where did the fish come from?"

"Pa went to the stream and brought back many fishes."

"A lot of fish, Abby. Say it. Pa brought back a lot of fish."

"Pa brought back a lot of fish," the little girl said happily. "See, I am learning my lessons very fast. And Ma, Pa has been helping us with our homework today."

"Is that right?"

"Yes, Ma," Mary sighed exaggeratedly. "But he does not know how to teach like you, Ma."

"Traitor," William said in mock anger, waving a fist at Mary who giggled, and her sister joined her.

As usual when supper was over, the family gathered in the sitting room for their devotions. William as usual sat on the porch and listened as they sang and prayed. When they were done he stepped into the room.

"Miss Elizabeth, may I speak with you?" He stepped back

outside and Elizabeth followed him. He waited for her to sit in her usual chair.

"I just want to say that I am sorry."

"That is okay." She looked at her hands.

"No, it is not okay. I know how much you have sacrificed to be here, and I should have made things a little easier for you." William shook his head in self-disgust. "Instead, I have added onto your troubles. Please forgive me." He came to stand in front of her and then he crouched so he could see her face in the dusky evening. His hands reached for hers, which were on her lap, and he touched her blisters gently. "I am sorry that I have not been a good husband to you, Miss Elizabeth. I will get you some ointment for these painful blisters when I go to town tomorrow."

"It is alright. I also want to ask you to forgive me for interfering with Amelia's things, without your permission."

"There is nothing to forgive. I thank you for waking me up to reality." He stood up again. "It is not easy to forget someone you loved."

"Mr. William, no one is asking you to forget Amelia. She will always be a part of your life, especially because of Mary and Abigail. You have those memories, and they are what God gives us when our loved ones leave us. He allows us to have pleasant memories, and remember the good times that we shared, and that helps us face tomorrow, especially when we have the assurance that our loved ones are in heaven with the Lord. We are then sure that we will one day be with them."

William did not want to hear anything about God and he decided to change the topic. "Tomorrow, I will put the trunks here in the sitting room, so that you can sort out what can be adjusted to fit the girls, and what can be used for the house." He sighed. "This is your house now, Miss Elizabeth, and I am sorry that I have not accorded you the respect you deserve as my wife, and as the lady of the house. You are free to make any changes that you want."

CHAPTER SEVEN

The crescent moon cast long shadows and the lone figure rode, casting furtive glances over her shoulder. Virginia hoped no one had heard or seen her leave the house. She was very excited and urged the horse to go faster. She had become skilled at handling Spitfire, and the horse obeyed her every command.

This was the first time she was leaving the house in the middle of the night, at least here in Missoula. In Boston she had done it all the time and Elizabeth had been none the wiser. She smiled a secret smile.

The other day while on one of her long rides with Spitfire, she had ridden into Hellgate and had gone to Reveler's Saloon, a tavern run by a heavily made-up woman who spoke with a French accent. She had slipped in and waited to see if anyone would notice her. The revelers were busy with their drinking and women, and at first no one paid any attention to her.

But Madam Belle had a keen eye and always noticed strangers amongst her customers. She had spotted Virginia and sent one of her girls to call her.

"The madam wants to see you," a girl her own age told Virginia. "Come with me, without a fuss." Virginia smiled and followed her to a back room. Madam Belle observed the young girl, whose eyes she had noticed lit up when she saw money.

"This can be an easy prey," Belle thought.

"What are you doing here, child?"

"I sing, and I was wondering if you can give me a job as a singer."

"What can you sing?"

"Everything. Okay, at least a number of songs. You see, in Boston…"

"Boston? You are from Boston?"

"Yes, ma'am."

"Where did you sing in Boston?"

"At the Wild West Tavern," Virginia said. "Can I sing for you?"

"Go ahead."

Virginia did a rendition of 'The Wisconsin Emigrant,' and because she was so passionate about her singing, the girl did the song with gestures, and when she was done Madam Belle clapped the loudest. This girl would fetch her good money.

"Honey, when can you start working, or shall I say singing, for Revelers' Tavern?"

"I got the job?"

"Yes indeed." Madam Belle pulled the girl to her buxom chest and hugged her. "You and me, princess, will make the bucks here in Hellgate. We will make a lot of money every day."

Virginia's face fell. "I am sorry, ma'am. I cannot come every night. I have to help out on the farm, and it gets pretty tiring. But I can come in two nights a week to start, and when my folks get extra help, I can come in every day."

Madam Belle swallowed a retort. Let the child come in and get a little money. Her own greed will have her coming back for more. The lure of the good life and good money was too strong for most, and she had seen the way the girl looked at the money that was brought to her.

"Before you go, can you sing for my guests? I will pay you two dollars."

"Two whole dollars?" Virginia's eyes lit up. "Yes, I will sing."

And so it was that she was going to sing on the stage tonight: this was her first night. And it turned out to be a huge success because Madam Belle had spread word around that she had fresh blood coming in, and as usual the miners with money to burn came to see what new thing the French madam had for them.

They unanimously agreed that Virginia had a lovely voice and she kept them entertained with many songs, but when it was almost dawn she had to leave. Madam Belle handed her ten dollars and the girl's eyes almost popped out.

"That one is a greedy one," Madam whispered to one of her girls. "She will soon be discontent with the singing wages and want some more, and when she does, I will be ready. Virgins fetch a very high price, indeed." The two women smiled slyly at each other.

When Virginia got home no one had stirred, and she made pretense of having been out running the horse.

~~ *** ~~

Elizabeth smiled when she thought about her daughters. These two girls were the children of her heart and she was growing to love them so deeply, and they loved her back. They were very obedient, and what made Elizabeth cry was when Abigail began to grow back her hair and wear dresses like her sister. And Mary had stopped the ritual of placing her mother's cup on the table during meals and putting it back once the meal was over. They were adjusting to the loss of their mother very nicely, like normal children do.

Getting Abigail to wear dresses had been a tough war indeed.

She would pretend to wear a dress, but when she got to school she would take it off to reveal dungarees. Mary was not a snitch, but she always told her sister that she was sinning against their new mama.

"Please don't tell Mama. I don't want to hurt her, but I hate dresses."

"I won't tell on you because I don't want to hurt Mama, but I wish you would stop this, Abby."

Elizabeth knew that the young girl wore boys' clothes under her regular school clothes, but she gave her time, and enticement. Elizabeth found beautiful frocks in Amelia's trunks and she adjusted them to fit the girls. Because William was around a lot in midsummer, Elizabeth did not have so much work to do and devoted the time to beautifying the house.

She made quilts for all their beds, assisted by the girls. They also made pretty curtains for all the rooms, including William's. Each day she made a dress each for the girls, including Virginia, and after supper but before they had their devotions, she would have them model the dresses for their father. Slowly, Abigail began loving her dresses. She saw the pretty ribbons that Elizabeth made for Mary's hair and also desired to keep her hair long. This was a great achievement for Elizabeth, and she was smiling as she put her violin away for the evening.

"What is making my dear wife smile this evening?" William asked when she joined him on the porch, as the girls prepared for bed.

"Abby. She is taking to ribbons and dresses like a duck to water."

"All thanks to you, Miss Elizabeth." William touched her cheek gently and Elizabeth was stunned. He had not made such a gesture to her before, and as though he realized what he was doing, he pulled his hand back quickly. "You are a good mother, and I am happy that you came to us, Miss Elizabeth."

"And thank you, Mr. William, for giving us a home. I am truly grateful."

"Didn't you have anyone else back in Boston who could have taken care of you after your father died?"

"No." Elizabeth shook her head sadly. "Papa was an only child and had no relatives, and Mama's relatives disowned her when she chose to marry Papa who those English called a commoner, and yet she was betrothed to a lord or baron, something like that. It was a man with a title."

"I am sorry."

"That is alright. At least we had each other."

"Was your papa from England also?"

"His grandparents were Irish, but Papa was born in Boston."

"How did he and your mama meet?"

"Papa was a businessman, and on one of his travels abroad he met Mama when his hosts in England took him to the opera. For them it was love at first sight, and they had a good marriage for ten years." Elizabeth sighed. "When Mama died, it was as though the life was snuffed out of Papa. He made bad business deals as a result of being absent-minded, and that is why when he died, we lost everything." She put her head to her side. "I think he suffered the heart attack because creditors were putting pressure on him, and he had no money."

"That is very sad, Miss Elizabeth."

"But God has been my strength all through, Mr. William. That is why I have been able to go on. I lost my mama when I was only nine and then my papa just recently, and everything we own. It was easy to give up, but God gave me the strength to go on, and in His divine mercy, He made a way out for us."

"Was it that bad?"

Elizabeth nodded. "I don't want Virginia to know that I know, but when we were in Boston she began to sneak out of the room where we lived, and one day I followed her and found her singing in a very shady tavern."

"What did you do?" William was horrified, imagining all sorts of things.

"I prayed, and God led me to look for a husband, and that is why I began communicating with you."

"But from the time that you first wrote to me, until you were able to come here, was about two and a half months. Did Virginia continue singing in those places?"

"Not for long. You see, she was struck down by an illness, and the doctor said it was an inflammation of the lungs. She was bedridden for about a month, and even when she got better she was too weak and could not go out. And that was when you sent us the money. As soon as I got the money, I booked our tickets, and we were out of there."

"That was very sad. Why would Miss Virginia want to go down that road?"

"When Papa was still alive, she believed that she would be a famous singer and travel the world. And she was getting ready for her coming out party which would have introduced her to society, and fame, she hoped also. And she hoped to find a rich suitor to finance her dream."

"I understand now."

"It was a big blow for her when Papa died, and all her dreams died with him. So I really understand what she was going through. I was just glad to get her out of that world. At least here I know she will be okay. This is a lovely place, away from all temptations, and I am hoping that soon she can meet a fine young man and become a wife and mother."

"Miss Virginia is welcome to live here with us for as long as she wants, and can, until she finds her own place."

"Thank you, Mr. William."

"You are welcome, Miss Elizabeth."

They sat in silence. "Mr. William, can I ask you something?"

"Yes, Miss Elizabeth."

"That scar, the one on the wrist of your right hand. How did you get it?"

He chuckled, rubbing the scar. "I tried my hand at cooking, and this was the badge of honor that was bestowed on me for my feeble attempts."

"I am sorry." She hid her smile.

"Ah! No need to be. It was about a month after Amelia died. We had finished all the food that the parishioners had brought us, and we were hungry. And Kate had gone back to her home, so I tried using that stove. It taught me a lesson I will never forget."

Over the days Elizabeth began to feel as though things were changing at home. William had brought his horses back and so spent less time away from home. When he was home, he was so attentive to her, and one time he borrowed Pastor Thomas' oxen wagon and took the girls to Hellgate for a day out as a treat, and also to pick up some supplies for the ranch. He left them to their own devices and returned a while later carrying a package which he put under the seat, offering no explanation as to what it was.

When they got back to the ranch he waited until the younger children and Virginia were in bed before he brought out his surprise package. They had maintained their talks on the porch every day after the evening devotions. William still did not join them, but sat on the porch as always, and once they were done with the prayers Elizabeth would join him on the porch, and they would talk for a long time.

William was pleased with his house. Once again, it was home: the smell of freshly baked breads and pies; his children's happy laughter; clean clothes; a nice-smelling bed. This was home, and he loved coming home.

"What is this?" Elizabeth received the package which was nicely wrapped in brown paper. She tried to guess what it was, but could not. It felt hard.

"Go on, open it."

She unwrapped the package and gasped when she saw what was inside. There were two pairs of blue long pants and she knew they would fit her. She had never seen such pants before.

"What are these, and where did they come from?"

"These are the new clothes that miners are now wearing. They are called 'denims' and they have just come out."

"Really? From where?"

"The shopkeeper said it is a certain German immigrant, who is in California, that we have to thank for these. His name is Levi Strauss. Mark my words, soon every cowboy or frontier woman you meet will be wearing these." He chuckled. "I intend to get all the girls some of those denims, too. They are good for working around the farm and riding."

"Thank you so much." The tears welled up in her eyes. This was such a kind gesture from William, and she felt like she was losing control over her resolution to keep this as a business arrangement.

"Hey, those are just working clothes. And besides, I bought them for you because I want to teach you how to ride astride a horse, and none of your clothes are appropriate for that."

"I don't know if I want to learn how to ride astride."

"It is important that you do. Sometimes you may want to go to town in a hurry, and that will get you there faster than if you sit side-saddle."

"Okay," she smiled, and his heart almost stopped when her dimples showed. "You are very kind, Mr. William."

"And I also need to teach you how to handle a gun. Have you ever held a gun before?" Elizabeth shook her head.

"It is important for your safety and the girls, especially against coyotes and snakes. And sometimes we get some rough characters riding around. It is always good to be prepared."

It made sense to Elizabeth, and she was determined to learn whatever survival skills she needed to live in this new home of hers.

So it was that the next evening Virginia offered to prepare dinner and Elizabeth put on one of her new denims. She felt shy at the way it hugged her, so she put on a long loose frock over it, and William smiled when he saw her. Change for some people did not come easy.

She waited outside while he went into the stables to get the horses and, expecting him to bring her Misty, she was surprised when he led Primrose out instead.

"If you are okay with it, I would like for you to accept Primrose as your horse."

"Thank you." She looked at the horse with trepidation.

"Primrose is as gentle as Misty, only she is younger. Misty is too slow."

Elizabeth felt herself bonding with William over the coming days, and it began to scare her. She was falling in love with her husband and that was not the plan. This was supposed to be a business arrangement. She was not supposed to fall in love with William, and especially not when he was clearly still in love with his dead wife. How does someone compete with a dead person's spirit?

William taught her how to ride, and even though she was still afraid of the horses, she was learning how to cope. She had to if she was to survive in this place, because for the most part horses were the only means of transportation. She could get on and off her horse without assistance, though she still had to work on her speed. It took Virginia less than two minutes to get onto her horse but Elizabeth struggled, and if anyone was counting it would take her about ten minutes to get on to the horse.

William watched his wife in silent amusement and amazement. She was a feisty little thing and had a determined look in her eye each time they were out to practice more. She gradually learned how to handle a gun very well, and he knew that she would eventually be able to survive as a settler's wife.

Elizabeth held her shawl around her tightly as she went into the barn to collect the eggs that she knew her chicken had laid. She had earlier decided that she would leave some eggs so that they could hatch into chicks, and so increase the number of their poultry. She was careful when collecting the eggs, because the first time she had tried it the hens had pecked at her hands, and the painful lesson was a reminder of how mothers, whether human or animal or bird, will go to any lengths to keep their young ones safe.

It was early morning and she wanted to prepare an early breakfast, because William had told her last night that he would be riding around the property to check on the fence and ensure that it was secure as autumn was slowly approaching, even though the sun was still very hot during the day. Her mission accomplished, she returned to the kitchen and found her daughters and Virginia awake and setting the breakfast table.

"I need to go to Hellgate and stock up on some things," William announced during breakfast. "I will first ride around the farm to ensure the fence is secure, and then Pastor Thomas will be bringing his ox cart so we can all go to town. So ladies, put on your best frocks and join me on my trip." The loud cheers that welcomed his announcement warmed his heart. He had a family.

It was a wonderful trip to Hellgate, but Elizabeth noticed that her sister seemed uncomfortable and kept looking around, and at times would even duck.

"Virginia, what is going on? You look as though you are hiding from someone."

"Oh, it is really nothing. I am just being cautious because some of the men here are looking at me so much, and I do not want to attract any attention."

It was a lame explanation, but Elizabeth let it pass. She knew Virginia was still going through an adjustment period and did not want to make her feel uncomfortable in any way.

That evening after dinner as usual, the family held their prayers and Elizabeth played the violin. Virginia sang with them, but it was obvious that her mind was distracted. When the prayers were over the girls went to bed and as usual, Elizabeth joined William on the porch.

"Autumn is nearly here, Miss Elizabeth. I hope you have warm enough clothing, because the weather can be very chilly, not to mention winter."

"Thank you, Mr. William. I think we are all alright. The girls now have many dresses, which are of good material and will keep them warm."

"I meant you, my dear. Do you have sufficient clothing?"

"Yes, though I ran out of knitting yarn. I am making mittens for the girls and also a pair for you to keep out the cold."

"I would like to see that."

"I forgot to ask you to get me some yarn when we were in town today."

"Remind me to get you some when I go there tomorrow."

"Yes, Mr. William."

They sat in companionable silence for a while. Then Elizabeth shivered.

"Cold?"

"A little bit," she answered, drawing her shawl closer.

William moved from his position and joined her on the settee, which was made for two people, sat down next to her and pulled her close. Elizabeth almost groaned out aloud. His hard body felt so warm and so comforting. She wanted to close her eyes and stay there forever.

"Is that better?" he asked huskily.

"Yes," she whispered. She could feel his heart beating, a strong steady pulse that almost lulled her to sleep. This was a man that she could depend on, someone she could lean on. If only he were hers to have and to hold, in the real sense of the word. She sighed inwardly. She would not ask for more than he was willing to give. Just having a home for her and Virginia had made a big difference in their lives, and brought them the safety and security that they would not have found had they remained in Boston.

"Miss Elizabeth?"

"Mmmmmh?"

"Are you sleepy yet? Do you want to go in?"

"No, not yet. Just a little while more."

He drew her closer, and then he raised her chin gently with his right hand and she looked up at him, slightly confused. The full moon was rising and the sky was clear, not a cloud in sight. His breath smelled of mint. William liked to clean his teeth with a Eucalyptus twig each day and so his breath was always fresh.

Like a moth that was mesmerized by a flame, Elizabeth watched as William lowered his head slowly until his lips touched hers. No one had ever told Elizabeth what a kiss was like and she had never been kissed before, but when William put his lips on hers she gave a soft sigh and opened up to him.

William groaned and pulled Elizabeth closer as he deepened their kiss. Her breath was fresh and her soft lips were so enticing, and he felt long buried feelings begin to rise up in him again. A shudder rippled through him and he drew her even closer, both arms holding her close. She fit him so well, her softness against his hardness. And their kiss deepened even more. A thought came into his mind that this was his woman and he wanted to protect her, provide for her and be there for her

Elizabeth felt the heat rising up in her, chasing away the cold not only from her body, but from her heart as well. She felt protected and cherished and wished that this would go on forever, and that William would finally begin to need her as much as she needed him. She turned, put her arms around his waist, and held on to him.

Just when she was getting lost in the kiss, William stopped and pulled away. She felt his withdrawal not just physically, but emotionally as well, and her heart sank.

"I have got to go," he stood up abruptly.

"William…" she cried out softly.

"Not now, Miss Elizabeth, not now," and saying this he practically ran down the steps and a few minutes later Elizabeth heard him open the barn door and ride out.

"Oh!" She felt pain in her heart like never before. It was as though the very life was being squeezed out of her, and she closed her eyes and bent down as if in physical pain, moaning. She felt so rejected and abandoned, and her tears fell fast. This man would never come to love her in the way that she desired and she knew that eventually that reality would end up destroying her. She would have to get away and forget all about him. William would never love her, not while he was still in love with Amelia.

Elizabeth shook her head. She deserved the love of a good man, but she was not going to get it from William. She sat for a long while and then came to a decision. When it was daylight she would talk to William in the sobriety of the day, and tell him that she had decided to return to Boston. There she would live like a widow all the days of her life and never marry again, because she knew that what she felt for William was no youthful passion, but deep eternal love that would never end. She could never give her heart to another. William possessed it forever. He had slowly wound his way into her heart, soul and mind and taken permanent residence there, leaving no room for any other.

She shook her head sadly and stood up. Her tears had stopped but the pain in her heart was so deep. She did not get into bed, but sat on the stool beside her bed. She could hear Mary breathing softly on the other bed. Oh, to be young again and have no cares or pain in her life!

And then she heard something else. She listened keenly. It was the sound of the barn door opening again, and she frowned. She had not heard William riding back. She moved to the window which overlooked the stables, and in the moonlight she made out Virginia's form.

"What?" she whispered. As she watched, her sister led Spitfire out of range of the house and jumped on her and took off.

Elizabeth did not hesitate a moment longer, thankful that she had not taken off her denims yet. She ensured that Mary and Abigail were alright and asleep before she slipped out of the house and closed the door. She ran to the stables and got Primrose.

"Primrose, you and I have to go out this night, and I am sorry to disturb your rest," she whispered as she struggled to get on to the horse. "But we need to follow Virginia, and learn what she is up to. She could be getting herself into a lot of trouble." And, as if the horse understood her, she took off in the same direction that Virginia had gone.

"Father," Elizabeth prayed as she held on tightly to the reins. "Please guide my footsteps so that I can find my sister, before she gets into trouble and ruins her life. Protect us from every form of evil, and protect the children, too. In Jesus' name, I pray. Amen."

CHAPTER EIGHT

William got off Black Thunder and tethered the horse to a tree. It was chilly but he did not feel it. He was quite agitated by the different emotions that were filling him. How could he have betrayed Amelia like that? He had promised her as she lay dying that he would never love another woman. She would always have his heart. And now he had betrayed that love and trust and he clicked in self-disgust. He walked to her grave and stood looking down at it.

He tried to remember Amelia's face, but all he could come up with was Elizabeth's chubby and dimpled face, and her full heart-shaped lips, her innocent eyes as she blinked at him from behind her glasses whenever she was reading and had them on. He closed his eyes and groaned. The woman had taken his wife's place in his mind as well.

William walked around the clearing, the bright moon lighting up the clearing where he was. He loved this spot because whenever he was troubled he could come here and feel at peace. He rubbed his five o'clock shadow with his right hand, his left hand at his waist. Black Thunder stood by, watching him. As William paced, he felt as though all the creatures were watching him. It did not frighten him in any way. If anything, it filled him with something he could not explain: a deep sense of oneness with the universe and nature.

The gentle breeze made the leaves rustle in the night, leaves that would soon be shed as autumn arrived. The soft humming of night insects sounded like a song to William. He smiled and closed his eyes, and he knew what Elizabeth had felt when she had first seen the mountains: a sense of reverence and awe.

For the first time in a long while he felt deep peace taking over his heart. And he heard Pastor Thomas' voice, as the clergyman had spoken to him a few weeks after Amelia's death.

"There is no pain like the pain of losing someone you love so deeply, but even with the pain of death comes the knowledge that because our loved ones loved the Lord, they are now in His presence, and their pain is gone."

"Why is God so cruel, Pastor Thomas?" William was full or rage and grief. "If He is as loving as you claim, why does He allow pain like this? Amelia was a young woman with small children. Why would God do something like this and deny these children their mother, when they still need her? And what about me? Does your God care for me, too? Or is this a way of punishing me?"

"No William, you have got it all wrong." The older man sighed. "There are some questions whose answers we will never know until we cross over to the other side. But one thing that I know for sure is that in all things, God is working for our good, and no matter what we are going through, if we believe that God is right there with us, it makes the pain bearable."

William did not say a word.

"There is a season and time for everything under the sun. For some of us our sojourn here on earth is for a long time, for others, like Sister Amelia, it is a short one. But the truth is that life must go on. You must go on, William, for the sake of your children, Mary and Abigail."

William looked at Pastor Thomas. "And what is that supposed to mean?"

Pastor Thomas chuckled. "You are young, William. You are a strong young man who can sire many more children."

"Amelia is dead."

"Indeed, she is dead. But when the time comes, your heart will open up to someone else."

"Never!"

"William," the older man put his hand on William's sleeve, "I may not understand exactly how you feel, but I know the pain of loss and of thinking that there is no way a person can go on. In my fifty-five years of life and thirty years as a pastor, I have seen people come and go, children born, children dying before adulthood. I have buried fathers and mothers, and have shared pain with many of my congregants. And one thing I can tell you is that things will never be the same again. Life changes after the loss of a loved one. It becomes different. God has given us the ability to cope with whatever comes our way, but only if we entrust ourselves into His loving arms. It does not get easier, it just becomes different. And when the right time comes, allow your heart to open up and let someone else in."

"That is betraying Amelia."

"No, no, no, my son. Betrayal is if you should love another while your wife is still alive and you are together. The Bible says that once a wife or husband is dead, the remaining spouse has been set free, and can move on and love someone else again."

William sighed. He looked around him and once more was caught up in memories.

"William," Pastor Thomas said, "moving on to love someone else is part of the cycle of life. Look at the trees. In winter they lie frozen beneath the ice. Spring comes and they thaw, and new life begins. Then summer comes and they are in the prime of their life, not knowing that autumn is just around the corner, when they will have to shed all their leaves and bow down once again to the weight of snow in winter. Such is life. Even when it is bleak like winter, spring comes, and life becomes new again. Do you understand what I am saying?" William nodded.

"You can be sure that when life ends, new life begins. For our sister, life has ended on this side of heaven, but it has begun in paradise where she is beholding the face of our Savior and Lord, Jesus Christ. For you and the children, life with Amelia has ended. But it can begin again when you move on and find another woman to bring you and the children comfort. No one can ever take the place of your wife, but you can make room for someone else. That is how big our hearts are, and we never know it until we have to go through something like this."

At the time William had thought the older clergyman rather mad, but now it all made sense to him. He was not betraying Amelia in any way by opening his heart to Elizabeth. Amelia was a part of his life that would always be there, and he did not need to hold her image in his mind always, because through their children she would always live. She was in Mary's eyes, in Abigail's smile.

For the first time in a long time William smiled from the heart. Yes, he would not forget Amelia, never, but he could open up his heart and love another, Elizabeth to be precise. And he realized that his new wife was a very honorable woman. He had overheard a conversation between her and Mary. They were in the barn collecting eggs and had not realized that he was in the stable grooming the horses.

"Mama?"

"Yes, my beautiful child?"

"I miss my mama."

"I know you do, little one, I know you do. I also miss my mama a lot."

"I am afraid."

"Why, Mary? What is making you afraid?"

"That I will forget her, and that makes me sad."

Elizabeth put down her basket of eggs and pulled the child in for a hug. "When our loved ones die in the Lord, they go into His very presence, and are happy with Him there until we join them. Do you understand that?"

"Yes, Mama."

"And even though we have a lot of pain here, God has given us a precious gift that we can never lose."

"What is that, Mama?"

"Memories. The memories we shared with our loved ones live in our hearts, and whenever we feel sad, we can always remember the good times and things that we did, that will put a smile on our faces."

"Mama?"

"Yes, child?"

"I love you, and I am so glad that Mrs. Thomas helped me to put that advert in the paper, and you and Papa fell in love, and Papa married you, and now you are our mama."

"And baby, I love you too, and I am also glad that I am your new mama."

William smiled and walked to Black Thunder. It was time to go home, time to go to his wife, time to start a new cycle of life. He paused at Amelia's grave before he got onto his horse. "Amelia, you know how much I loved you. I still do, and I always will. And the fact that I am going to build a new life with Elizabeth does not mean that you are out of my life. You will always be in my life and my heart, and in our children I see you everyday."

He jumped onto his horse and urged Black Thunder home. He was going to finally make things right with Elizabeth, his wife, tonight. He opened the stable door and urged Black Thunder in, not going in to check if all was alright. Black Thunder would find his own way to his stall. There were more important things for him to do right now.

He strode purposefully towards Amelia's old room and opened the door. The moonlight lit the room and as his eyes adjusted themselves, he frowned. Elizabeth's bed was empty. In fact it showed no signs of having been slept in. He quickly went to the porch where he had left her. It was empty, too. Then something struck him and he went to the room that Virginia shared with Abigail. Her bed was empty too.

William's heart constricted in fear. "Oh Lord, what have I done?" He secured the front and back doors and rushed outside to the stables, and his fear deepened. Primrose and Spitfire were missing, which meant that the two girls had left.

William felt like his heart was being ripped out of his chest. He shook his head. It was all his fault. He had driven away the one woman who had brought his household, his children and now, he finally admitted, his own life into order. She was probably on her way back to Boston because she believed he did not love her.

He had kissed her and left her high and dry on the porch, and ridden away with no explanation. William sighed. What a selfish person he had been. Elizabeth had left her life behind her and come to join him on the ranch, and over the weeks she had showed him what a wonderful woman she was. And he knew that she loved him. Otherwise, she would not have responded to his kiss in the way that she had. She was a rare woman, a precious woman, and he had lost her because of being very stubborn. She was valuable, but he had treated her like she was of no importance to him. That must have hurt her so badly, and he felt deep pain in his heart. He loved Elizabeth. He could finally admit that. He was in love with her.

Then his jaws tightened. He shook his head once again. He was not going to lose Elizabeth, not without a fight. With that resolve, he ran back into the house and got his rusty rifle and jumped onto Black Thunder. They could not have gone very far because he knew Elizabeth was still not yet fully confident of riding, and especially not in the dark. But they had about a two hour head start on him. He smiled. No problem there. Black Thunder was a powerful horse and faster than both Primrose and Spitfire, and he would soon catch up with the ladies.

"Lord," he prayed, for the first time in a long time. "Please show me the way."

CHAPTER NINE

Jeffrey Douglas spat on the ground before him. He was addicted to chewing tobacco, which had blackened his teeth over the years. He was six-feet tall, and well-muscled due to the long hours that he spent on his horse and rounding up the livestock that he and his boys stole from farmers around Missoula County. They would then drive the animals a long way to sell them to unsuspecting buyers who never realized that they were buying stolen goods.

He looked around at his three men and grinned. This was his pride and joy: his gang. And they were good. He was in a good mood because they had hit a farm earlier in the evening and made off with twenty head of cattle. Good, fat, healthy cows that would fetch him a good price with his buyers. As always, he had first ensured that none of the cattle had any branding marks on them.

The 'Hellgate Gang.' That was how people referred to them, though no one knew who they were. And he was mighty proud of the name and what he had achieved so far. His papa would be mighty proud of him, too. After all, it was the old coot who had initiated him into being a cattle rustler. But the old man had slowed down with age, and two years ago had been gunned down by the sheriff, in an operation that had gone bad. Initially, the gang had consisted of ten men but after that unsuccessful raid, where five of the men had been gunned down, including his father, Jeffrey had the option of recruiting more bandits to join him, but he realized that keeping a large group of cutthroats contented was not easy.

Because the men were always on the run from the law, tempers were always high and there was a lot of tension. Fights broke out easily among them and sometimes they even fought over the spoils of their raids.

Jeffrey spat again. No, he had done the right thing and only kept three men with him. These three he could control because he easily intimidated them. They were afraid of him, and Jeffrey had learned that the best way to keep his men in line was to instill deep fear in them, so that none would ever double-cross him.

"I can hit a can at fifteen paces, with one eye closed," he often bragged to his men. "So don't none of you get it into your heads to double-cross me."

The men were wary of him because he had an easy right hand that could shoot out unawares and do a lot of damage to the recipient of the blow. They had seen Jeffrey beat a man to a pulp with his bare hands, and they tended not to argue with him when he was in a foul mood.

He was a fighter, and through his thirty-nine years he felt that he had always been fighting. Born of a bandit and a whore, during the first years of his life he had lived with his mother in the brothel where she operated from, in Helena. She had been a pretty but wasted woman who had died of a wasting disease when he was fifteen. But before she died she had told him about his father. Immediately after the burial he had gone in search of his father.

At first Bud Douglas had resented his son's presence, thinking the boy was just there to sponge off of him. Bud had been a selfish and cruel man, and his own gang were restless and discontented, because even after successful raids he gave them only a small share of the booty. When Jeffrey had found his father, he had proved himself loyal by fighting off four gang members who had risen in mutiny against Bud. The result was that he got his two front teeth knocked out, but he had killed two of the men with his bare hands. The other two were shot by his father, and the four bodies dumped in an abandoned mine.

"Hey, boss?"

"Yes, Dusty?"

"The cattle are secured," Dusty informed him.

"Good. Now we can go and have us some fun, get us some wenches to warm our beds," he grinned at his gang members, and they cheered. The gang consisted of himself, Dusty, who was his right hand man and with whom many wars had been fought. Like Jeffrey, Dusty was thirty-nine years old, blond with blue eyes, six feet tall and very handsome. He usually was the decoy. Dusty would ride up to a farm or ranch and use his good looks to charm and seduce the maids, and once in a while the daughters or wives, of the farmers. From them he would gather secrets on how the farm was run, the security in place and, once he got this information he would pass it on to the gang, and they would then strategize and make a hit, often very successfully.

Then there was Lovejoy, a thirty-five year old man who had come to Montana during the gold rush. No one knew why he called himself Lovejoy, and he never volunteered the information. He was originally from Ohio and had lost all his savings and earnings to unscrupulous traders, and had turned to petty theft to survive. That was until he met Jeffrey, who recruited him into the gang.

Finally there was Roy, a southerner who rarely spoke. He was thirty years old and, like Lovejoy, had been a prospective miner. He had never had any luck finding anything of worth, and so had decided that he could help himself to other people's good fortune. He had been with Bud Douglas' gang, and when things had gone bad he had fled with Jeffrey, Lovejoy and Dusty, and they had become a gang.

Their hiding place was a large abandoned silver mine, and the overgrowth hid the entrance from view. There was a second mine close by which they used as a storage space for the animals they stole during their raids, until they could get the animals out to prospective buyers. Like the first, this one was also hidden from view by large bushes.

"Let's go boys, can't keep the ladies waiting," Jeffrey spat once more and jumped onto his horse.

~~~ *** ~~~

"Father, please give me strength." Elizabeth slowly got off Primrose and patted her down. She had followed Virginia into Hellgate. She had lost sight of her sometime in the pursuit but Primrose had led her to Spitfire, who was tethered at the back of a tavern, and Elizabeth felt her heart almost breaking. Virginia was at it again.

"Lord, please show me what to do. Please help me," she prayed. Once she was sure the two horses were alright she surreptitiously made her way to the front side of the tavern. She heard Virginia singing and she pushed open the tavern door. The patrons were all captivated by Virginia's voice, and no one noticed the figure that slipped into the tavern.

Elizabeth was furious. There was her sister, dressed in a very tight dress and dancing seductively. She was wriggling her bottom and giggling as she sang, with men urging her on. Without giving a thought to her safety Elizabeth marched to the stage and grabbed Virginia by her arm.

"Let go of me," Virginia tried to shake off Elizabeth's hand, unsuccessfully. The Elizabeth in Boston would have let go because her hands were feeble then. Not this one. Working on the ranch had toughened her hands and arms and she held on.

"You are coming with me this instant, and will stop parading yourself like some loose, immoral woman."

"Leave me alone," Virginia cried, but that made Elizabeth all the more determined. She ignored all the heckling. Her one thought was to get her sister out of there. She dragged Virginia out. "Why are you always spoiling things for me," Virginia cried out. "I never asked to be brought to this forsaken place. You brought me here against my will, and now I want to live my own life."

"Life? Is this what you call life? Singing like a tramp in a common tavern?" She dragged her to the back of the tavern, to where the horses were waiting. "I promised Mama that I would look after you, and I have tried, Virginia. I took you out of Boston precisely because of this kind of thing." Virginia gave her sister a stricken look. "Yes, Ginnie, I followed you to the hell hole that you used to sneak to, and I saw you. And I prayed, and God struck you with an illness, and that is why I brought you here: to get you away from that evil life. Do you want to end up like a whore, when there is so much going for you? You have a good home and enough to eat. William may not be rich, but he provides for us very well, and he has a good reputation and would eventually find you a good husband. Do you think any good man will want you if they hear that you are singing in taverns, and allowing other men to paw you?" She glared at her sister, who had the grace to feel ashamed. "Is this the kind of life that you want for yourself? If it is, tell me, here and now, and I will let you go back and waste your life. And be sure that your sins will catch up with you, and because you have the mark of God upon your life, things will end very badly for you."

Virginia started crying. "I am sorry."

"That is not good enough. There is no use of saying you are sorry when you intend to go back to that house of sin and waste your life. If you are not coming with me, Virginia, you are no longer welcome to the farm, and I will wash my hands off of you. And much as I made a promise to Mama to always take care of you, I can only do so much. I am tired, Virginia. If you are willing to be helped, then I will stand by you no matter what, but if you want to waste your life, then I have done my best and you are free to leave." Elizabeth turned around to get Primrose.

"Elizabeth, I am sorry," Virginia wept. "I am so sorry. Please forgive me. Don't be mad at me. I have no one else but you left in this world, and if you turn your back on me, then where will I go?" Elizabeth sighed. "And please, do not tell William," Virginia pleaded. "I don't want him to be mad and send me away."

"Just get on the horse, and let us go home. We will talk about this when we get there."

"Ladies, ladies," a rough voice broke out in the darkness, and the two girls started. Jeffery and his gang rode into the yard and got off their horses. "What is the hurry? And the evening is very young!"

"Jesus, help us," Elizabeth whispered. "Lord, please come to our aid, we need you right now."

Jeffrey swaggered to the two ladies and stood in front of Elizabeth. He drew closer and she almost gagged. His breath smelled foul and he reeked of sweat, like someone who had not bathed in a long time.

"Hello there, my pretty," he lisped through the gap in his upper jaw. "You are a fine one for me." He pinched her cheek and she drew back and hissed at him. "Mmmh, a feisty one," he turned to his boys and they laughed. "It will be a joy to break this one in."

"Leave us alone," Elizabeth said in a shaky voice. "We are honorable women, and my husband is coming to get us."

"Oooh! I am scared," Jeffrey shook his hands in mock fear, causing his men to laugh out loudly. "What are you doing here at this time of night, if you are an honorable woman?" He reached out a hand and grabbed her curly hair.

"Just leave us alone." Elizabeth beat off his hand and stepped away from him.

"And why would I do that, when I have found me a good woman to keep my bed warm at night? Autumn is coming, and I do not want to get the chills. You will warm me very nicely." He swatted her bottom and she squealed.

The other three men were so intent on watching what their boss was doing that they paid no attention to Virginia, who slowly untied Spitfire's reins.

"Leave me alone," Elizabeth cried out. "The wrath of God will fall upon your head."

"Now, I am really scared," Jeffrey threw back his head and laughed. "Come, my beautiful, forget about your good for nothing limp snake of a husband, and come and warm my bed." He grabbed her hand.

"Let me go," Elizabeth struggled against Jeffrey, kicking him in the shin. "Let me go."

"Why you little…" he slapped her across the face and she reeled back and fell to the ground, where he threw himself on her, his evil intentions clear. He put his face in hers, his vice-like grip on her throat, and began choking her with one hand as the other fumbled with her clothes.

"Boss, there is some people coming," Dusty called out as they heard loud voices. The three men knew what their boss was capable of, and even though they also enjoyed ravishing women whenever they got the chance, this was not the place. They fell on him to drag him away, and that was the chance that Virginia was waiting for. She jumped onto Spitfire and dug his sides hard, and the horse shot off.

"Hey," Dusty called out, scrambling to his feet. That made Virginia all the more determined to get away and Spitfire thundered off into the darkness. Jeffrey stood up and dragged Elizabeth, who opened her mouth to scream, and he clamped a filthy hand over her mouth.

"Lord Jesus, save me," she prayed, terrified to death of what she knew the men would do to her. "Please send me help from Your sanctuary, oh Lord, for I trust in you."

Jeffrey flung her onto his horse and they quickly rode away. The men were laughing and making jokes.

"Boss, when you are done with the wench, I'm next," Dusty called out.

"Then me," Lovejoy said merrily.

"My turn will come," Roy said.

"He that dwells in the secret place of the Most High God shall abide under the shadow of the Almighty. I will say of the Lord, You are my refuge, You are my fortress. You are my God, and in You I trust. You will surely deliver me from this snare, Oh Lord.

Cover me with Your feathers and be my shield and buckler." Elizabeth closed her eyes and prayed, shutting out the voices of the men. She was lying across Jeffrey's horse and each step jarred her and made her stomach ache. And the smell of the animal, and the man on the animal, were enough to make her faint, but she refused to give in to fear. She would fight for her virtue. She would not go down without a fight.

"Lord, send Your angels to take charge over me and keep me. Guard my virtue, for I trust in You, and You alone. Deliver me, because I know Your name. I am calling upon you right now, please answer me. Deliver me and honor me, oh Lord. Do not let me be ashamed, do not let my enemies triumph over me."

CHAPTER TEN

"Lord, I am sorry," Virginia sobbed as Spitfire sped into the darkness. "Please forgive me for my selfishness, which has led my sister into grave danger." She had to get to William before those evil men harmed her sister. "Faster, Spitfire," she urged the horse. "You know Elizabeth is in grave danger. Please move faster."

She heard the sound of hoofs ahead and in the moonlight recognized William.

"William," she screamed, halting Spitfire.

William rode over quickly. "Virginia, what is wrong? Where is my wife? Where is Elizabeth?" William felt fear like never before. Virginia was sobbing harshly.

"They took her."

"They? Who are they?"

"Those evil men."

"Where were you when they took her?" he demanded, getting off his horse and approaching her. "What were you doing away from home?"

"I am sorry." Virginia's hands twisted the reins. "It is all my fault."

"What is your fault, Virginia? What are you talking about?" The story came pouring out and William's lips tightened. "Ride on home, and better pray that Elizabeth is safe," he said through clenched teeth. "If something happens to my wife because of your selfishness and carelessness, Virginia, I will never forgive you."

"I am sorry," Virginia said as she rode away.

William got onto Black Thunder but did not immediately begin riding. He had no idea who those evil men were because there were a number of gangs around Hellgate. It could be any of them. He felt so helpless and hopeless, and then he heard Pastor Thomas' voice:

"You can call upon God at any time of the day or night, and He will answer you. The Bible says that His ears are ever attentive to the cry of His children, and He will answer speedily. Call upon Him in the day of trouble, and see Him come through for you."

William looked up to heaven, then down again. He had turned his back on God and now he was in trouble, his love was in trouble, and there was nothing he could do about it. Unless a miracle occurred it would be too late by the time he found Elizabeth. He knew what gangs did to women that they kidnapped. Tales of horror were told, and he did not want to imagine that his sweet wife, the love of his life, would be ravished. It would destroy her and that was something that he could not live with. He had once seen a woman who had fallen victim to a gang. They had not only destroyed her body, but her soul as well, and the dead look in her eyes had been one that William would never forget. A few days later she had been found floating face down in the river, having ended her life. The pain was too much to bear.

William bowed his head. "Oh Lord," he groaned. "I am sorry. Please forgive me, Lord. Please forgive me." He begged. "For so long I turned my back on You, because I blamed You for Amelia's death. I walked away from You when I should have walked to You. It has taken the love and faith of a wonderful woman to make me realize that I have been very selfish in my life." He sobbed. "Elizabeth lost so much, but she kept her trust in You. She had to leave everything she loved behind, but her faith was unwavering. She has taken my children in and loved them like a mother, and I turned my back on her and denied her love and security. Lord, please forgive me, and help me find my wife before it is too late. She is Your servant, she has loved You with all her heart. Do not let these evil men destroy this beautiful woman. Please help me, God."

He was silent, and then was surprised when Black Thunder took off, almost unseating him. "Whoa there, Black Thunder," he said, when he was in control once more. The horse was practically flying and then came to a sudden halt.

William looked around him and saw an old trail. To an untrained eye it looked unused, but William got off his horse, thankful for the full moon which lit up the surroundings, and he could clearly see. He had spent time with Sure Foot who had taught him how to track, and he looked at the ground keenly. Horses had been this way. He saw something fluttering in the gentle breeze. It was a piece of cloth caught in the brambles. He took it and smiled, recognizing it. Yes, he was on the right trail. He made as if to get back onto the horse and then he paused. Right there on the trail, he knelt down.

"Father, I thank You for being merciful to me, and showing me the way. Take me back, oh Lord. I know that I am not deserving of Your mercy and grace, but please hear my plea, please cleanse me and renew me once again. Please lead me on and let me find my wife, the love of my heart, and the mother of my children. And Lord, please keep her safe. In Jesus' name I pray, amen."

Black Thunder was a sure-footed horse and that was why William loved riding him. He carefully picked his way on the trail, stopping from time to time to get his bearings right. He had been riding for almost an hour when he sensed Black Thunder tensing up. There was an eerie silence and he knew great fear. He knew he was nearing his destination, whatever he sought, and he slid off the horse and knelt down again.

"Lord Jesus, I come to You at this moment. I am so scared, not only for my life, but for my wife's life. You have led me this far, I submit to You now." He wiped his tears. "I am before You on my knees, and I finally surrender to Your will. Have Your way in my life from this moment onwards. I give myself to You, Lord. Help me, please help me."

He got back to his feet and held Black Thunder by the reins, leading him. There was a clearing ahead and he could hear men jeering and laughing. He peered between the trees and saw one of the men struggling with someone. He knew it was Elizabeth. Once again hopelessness and helplessness filled him and he bowed his head again.

His Elizabeth was a virgin. She was a virtuous woman who had kept herself pure, even in the midst of her suffering in Boston. A lesser woman might have given in to temptation, all to secure her future, but not his wife. And she had come to him as a pure woman, untouched, unblemished, a precious gift to a husband. Her purity would have been a precious sealing of their marriage covenant. But he had not esteemed her, nor valued her, and now her life was about to be changed and destroyed.

On his way back from Amelia's graveside in the woods, he had been thinking and come to the decision that loving Elizabeth was the right thing to do. He had decided that tonight would be the night when they would share their love. He knew Elizabeth would give herself willingly to him because he loved her, and he knew that she loved him. He had smiled as he thought about consummating their love, how he would be the first man to touch her, and how he would teach her not to be afraid of him or of their love.

But now it was not to be. He shook his head. He was sure that the men would take it in turns to destroy his beautiful wife's body, but at this moment he did not care. As long as they did not kill her he would help her heal both in mind and body because she belonged to him, with him for eternity. She was his treasure and no matter how much treasure was trampled upon, it never lost its value. They would hurt her body, but he would be there to help her heal.

He knelt down for one more prayer.

~~~ *** ~~~

The bandits reached their hideout and the Jeffrey jumped off his horse, dragging Elizabeth off the animal, and she fell like a heavy sack to the ground. He laughed. He tried to drag her towards the cave, but she struggled and he let go. The other three men tied their horses and prepared to have fun with the woman that they had captured.

"You will make a mighty fine woman for some time," he spat on the ground. Elizabeth lay unmoving on the ground and he swooped in and hurled her to her feet. His foul breath and bodily smell overcame her, and she retched and soon emptied the contents of her stomach on his shoes. He made a sound of disgust and dropped her once again.

"Get up," Jeffrey shouted at her. "Get up woman, or I will shoot you this instant." He was pointing a shotgun at her and she bowed down and began to sob.

Jeffrey looked at her and shook his head. This was a really stubborn one and he would break her in, and he would have fun doing so. But first he wanted to check on the cows to see if the gang's property was secure. Other gangs often trailed them, trying to steal their booty from time to time. The woman was alright for now. She was going nowhere, helpless as a kitten.

"Watch her," he called out to Dusty, and put his shotgun back in his saddle and turned his back. He did not know that Elizabeth had been praying for an opening, and when he had taken a few paces away from her she jumped up, fear and adrenaline giving her the strength she needed, and snatched the gun from the horse's saddle.

Jeffrey turned in disbelief when he heard the gun being cocked. He took a step forward and Elizabeth raised the gun and fired into the air. He stepped back hastily. She looked at the other three who had left their horses a distance away. None of them had their weapons on them.

She knew how to aim and she could shoot straight, thanks to the hours of practice she had had with William. She squinted in the moonlight, wishing she had her glasses, and raised the gun, anger making her desire for revenge. These men had done evil to a lot of women and she was not going to be a victim. She would shoot them all. Then she shook her head. God would send her help just in time. She had that assurance in her heart. She would not kill them. Their time would come and they would die, but not at her hands.

~~~ *** ~~~

"Father, all strength is with You. You are the all powerful and all mighty God. You know what these evil men intend to do to my wife. I am helpless, and I do not know what to do. I am crying to you at this time. Hear me from heaven, Oh Lord, and answer me. Shield my wife, for she is the love of my heart. She is my portion from You, only I was too selfish and proud to acknowledge it before, but now I do. Please Lord, let it not be too late for Elizabeth, for us. In Jesus' name…"

Before he could say his amen he heard a shot and quickly peered in the direction from which it had come. And a smile broke out on his face. His beautiful wife held a shotgun and she looked threatening indeed.

"I am prepared to shoot the first man who dares to come close," he heard her voice. "And make no mistake, I will not miss. My husband is an excellent marksman and he taught me how to shoot, so if you are daring enough, come close."

William looked ahead of him. He counted four men in all. His keen eyes looked around to see if there were possibilities of there being more men, but soon realized these four were who he needed to contend with. He quickly got onto his horse. He knew that it was just a matter of time before the bandits jumped Elizabeth and overpowered her. She had the upper hand right now, and another woman would already have shot and killed or maimed her abductors, but he knew his wife had so much compassion in her heart that she would not kill the men. He made one last prayer.

"Greater is the army of the Lord that is with us, than they are," he murmured. "Lord, send Your mighty army to fight for Elizabeth this night, in Jesus' name, I pray, amen." And he released Black Thunder to begin her trot into the clearing ahead, careful not to expose himself to the bandits. He had seen the three horses and made for them to cut the bandits off from reaching them. He went around until he was between the men and their animals.

"Boss, do you hear that?" Roy looked around him in fear.

"Sounds like horses to me," Lovejoy agreed. "Many horses, and they are headed this way."

Jeffrey spat on the ground. "You be shaking like old women when you hear the rustling of the wind. Idiots." He took one step forward towards Elizabeth and hastily jumped back when a shot rang out and a bullet grazed the dust at his feet. Dusty, Lovejoy and Roy fled back in terror.

"I come in peace," William called out in a voice that sent the chills down the backs of the four bandits. "All I want is my wife. I have no interest in what you are about. Just release my wife to me."

"Who are you?" Jeffrey tried for boldness.

"Remember Henry Plummer?" William said, and the four men took a further step backwards, away from Elizabeth. "My sister-in-law has gone to get the sheriff, and they are riding fast behind me. You all know what that means. You will be strung like Henry Plummer and his gang, but I am prepared to let you all go, on condition that you release my wife."

The bandits held a hurried discussion. Jeffrey, and indeed the whole gang, had heard of Henry Plummer. Ten years had passed but the story still brought terror into the hearts of all who heard it, and especially those who were on the wrong side of the law.

Henry Plummer had been a handsome and charismatic man who was chosen by the Bannack community then to be the sheriff, but unknown to them he was also the leader of a gang who robbed and killed miners, and snatched their gold and other possessions. But their luck had run out when the settlers got tired of the killings and robberies. This was especially after one gang killed a well-liked Dutchman, called Nicholas Thiebalt. The outrage had led to the formation of vigilante groups, and one such group captured Henry Plummer and his two deputies when investigations pointed to them as being the ring leaders of the gangs, and the three were hanged without a trial.

Jeffrey swallowed hard. If the sheriff was on his way, it only meant one thing. There would be trouble, and especially when he remembered that the livestock in the second cave would be a dead giveaway. And the sheriff did not ride alone. He had a group of people with him, and no doubt people seeing the sheriff riding out would be interested, and there would be many others following, some of who might be the dreaded vigilante. And the sheriff was half Nez Perce, and was known to be a very keen tracker. This same sheriff had killed his father and part of their gang two years ago, and had been searching for Jeffrey. The bandit shook his head.

The vigilante spared no one. They had been known to snatch bandits from the sheriff as they were being taken to trial, and hang them without a trial, and Jeffrey wanted none of this. Life was precious. He was not about to lose all he had worked for, just for a mere slip of a woman.

"If you let us go, I will lead the sheriff away from you," William said. "Time is running out, and I need your answer, or else it will be too late."

"Ah, take your woman and be gone," Jeffrey spat. "More trouble than she is worth."

William smiled. "Elizabeth, come to me." He kept his gun well trained on the four bandits as he watched his wife running towards his voice. "Come to the trees towards the horses," he urged, and she ran faster, the shotgun still in her hands. She was not taking any chances.

When she got to William, he reached out a hand and hoisted her up behind him. She dropped the shotgun.

"Okay now?" he asked gently.

"Yes," she whispered, clutching his waist with both arms and holding on for dear life. Her face was hidden on his back. He smelled so nice, so fresh, after the foul smell she had had to endure for hours.

William fired his rifle towards Jeffrey once again to disorient him and the bandits scattered, then he turned Black Thunder and they rode off.

CHAPTER ELEVEN

Virginia was too agitated to sit still. She kept pacing in front of the house, her tears falling. "Lord, please forgive me. Please let Elizabeth and William be safe," she repeated over and over again. Then she heard the sound of hoofs and sat down quickly on the step, just as William rode up to the house, Elizabeth clinging to his back.

He got off the horse and helped his wife down. She clung to him, still shaking from her ordeal.

"I am so sorry," Virginia ran to her sister, who shrank from her and clutched at William. "I am so sorry, Elizabeth."

William ignored her and held his trembling wife in his hands. She needed to know that she was safe and had nothing more to fear. "You are safe now, my love," he whispered into her ear, and Elizabeth thought she had heard him wrong. "There is nothing to fear now."

Gradually the trembling ceased and William knew the worst of it was over. He released her from his hug but kept her close to his side and then turned to Virginia, his features stern and clearly visible to Virginia in the bright moonlight.

"Of all the selfish things to do, Virginia, this was the worst. How could you be so stupid as to put my wife's life in danger like that? Not to mention your own? Do you hate being here that much? Mmmh? Answer me," he demanded.

"I am sorry."

"You better be. If you feel this is not the place that you want to be, then when it is daylight pack your things and leave my home. You will not put my wife or my children's lives in danger, all because you feel you must shine. I understand that you have lost your dreams and everything you hoped to achieve, but you can find new dreams and a new life, just not as a whore."

Virginia held her head down in shame.

"Your sister lost so much more. And she sacrificed her life to bring you here, so that you would begin life anew, and is this how you repay her? By running off to shame yourself, and her, in front of drunks and bandits?" He clicked in disgust. "You think you are the only one who lost all you had? Have you ever stopped to consider your sister for just one moment? She cleans after you, and yet you are old enough to be doing that. She washes for you, cooks for you, looks after you as if you were a child, and yet you are a grown woman who will soon have her own home. Many nights your sister goes to bed quite exhausted, to wake up early and begin the cycle of work again, and you rarely help her. And when you do so, it is with a lot of grumbling."

Virginia raised a stricken face to her brother-in-law. She had never heard William this incensed before and she knew that she had crossed the line this time.

"Yes, I have heard you myself. Your sister serves you without complaining, and this is how you repay her? You better thank God that I found her just in time, before anything bad happened to her, or else you would have paid for everything, Virginia. You would have paid dearly."

"I am so sorry, it will never happen again, and I promise with my whole heart." The girl was in deep anguish. Her sister would not even look at her.

"Pull yourself together and get your life back on track, or else I will send you out of here and do not imagine that I will not. This time you went too far and almost brought disaster to your own sister, who has been kind to you all your life. Can you imagine what would have happened to Elizabeth had I not reached her in time? Do you hate your sister that much, Virginia?"

"I am sorry."

"Go to bed, and let me think about what to do with you in the light of day. And do not take it upon your head to try and run away, because I will find you, and you will be sorry when I do. And in any case, if you want to leave then you can use your legs. Do not touch any of my horses, do you hear me?"

"Yes, sir," Virginia said in a trembling voice. "Elizabeth, I am sorry."

"Go on to bed." William barked, and she scrambled up the steps and into the house.

Elizabeth made as if to go to the house but William restrained her. "I know you are tired, and soon I will let you go and get some rest," William said as he led her to their spot on the porch.

"William," Elizabeth held out a hand to her husband. "I am so sorry on behalf of my sister. Please forgive her. She is a wayward child, but she has a good heart. I know that she will change. She can change."

"Well, she had better change, because the next time she tries something like this, I will not allow you to go after her and endanger your life."

"I know she is so scared, and will not dare again." She smiled sadly at her husband. "And thank you for risking your life to save me when you did not have to. I am sorry that we have been such a bother to you."

William made a choking sound and swiftly moved to Elizabeth.

"Look at me," he demanded softly and she raised tear-filled eyes to him. "You will never be a bother to me, Elizabeth," he whispered. "I love you so much."

Elizabeth gave a small cry and pulled back. "You don't love me," she turned her back on him, struggling with her tears. "You are still in love with your wife."

"It is true that I love Amelia, but I am in love with you and now it is different. Amelia will always be my first love." He had moved silently and held her by the shoulders and turned her around. "The difference is that you have my heart now, Elizabeth."

"But how? How do you know that it is me that you love, and I am not just a shadow of your wife?"

He smiled gently at her. "You are in my heart, in my mind, Elizabeth. When I am away from you, all I think about is you. You are the last person I think about before I fall asleep, you are the first person I think about when I am awake."

"Oh!" Elizabeth's tears rolled down her cheeks. William gently wiped them away.

"Tonight, when I realized that I could lose you, my heart felt as though it was breaking. I knelt down and recommitted my life to God, and prayed that He would protect you and keep you safe, and in His mercy, He heard my cry and delivered you out of the hands of those wicked men."

Just then they heard thundering hoofs and William reached for his rifle and kept it trained on the approaching intruders. Then he lowered it and chuckled.

"What?" Elizabeth looked up at him in confusion.

"It is only Primrose. I didn't see her at the camp."

"No, she got left at the tavern in town. I had tethered her. How did she break lose?"

"Someone must have untied her, probably with the intention of stealing her, when he saw that she was alone." He chuckled. "No one can steal my horses. They are crazy, and always find their way home."

Primrose stopped beside Black Thunder and the two horses began muzzling each other.

William turned his back to them and back to his wife.

"And I have finally found my way home, Elizabeth. I love you so much, and I want to say that I am sorry for not treasuring and cherishing you as I should have. My love, please forgive me."

"Oh, William," she put her head down, but he raised her chin.

"I declare my love for you, and I love you so deeply. It took a near disaster to wake me up to my real feelings, feelings that I have been trying to hide and battle for a long time now." He smiled at her. "When I lost Amelia, I vowed that I would never love another woman again, and no one would take her place. Then you came into my life, into our lives, and all that changed. My stubborn pride and stupidity refused to acknowledge what my heart was telling me, that I could love again. I actually selected you from a number of others because you sounded so businesslike, and did not seem to be someone who would interfere with my feelings. Little did I know that slowly, as I watched you love my daughters and take care of us and love us, that I would end up falling in love with you."

"Oh, William."

"And tonight, after we kissed, I had to flee because that was when I realized just how deep my feelings were for you. I felt as though I was betraying Amelia, but when I was in the woods everything became clear to me. This is a second chance that I have been given, and I was throwing it all away by being a stubborn fool. I hurried back to the house with the intention of telling you how I felt, and asking you to forgive me and give me a chance to show you how much I love you."

Elizabeth could not believe all she was hearing. She felt as though she was dreaming.

He dropped his hands and stepped away. "When I found you and the horses gone, I thought you had left me because I had not showed you how much you mean to me, how much I love you. I was coming after you to ask you, no, to beg you to come back to me. Then I met Virginia and she told me what had happened." His voice trembled, and Elizabeth reached out a soothing hand and laid it on his chest. "I thought I would die, especially when I realized that I could lose you. I prayed for you, Elizabeth, and I am so humbled that God honored my prayers and kept you safe." He stepped away from her and her hand fell to her side.

"I need to know, Elizabeth. I know you said you were not interested in marriage, in the true sense of the word, but do you have any feelings for me?"

Elizabeth smiled through her tears and her dimples showed. "William, I think I fell in love with you the first time I saw you, but I resisted and fought my feelings, because I could clearly see that you were still in love with your dead wife. I knew you were in a lot of pain, and I did not want to be bothersome to you."

William gave a happy cry and scooped her in his arms, and put his forehead to hers. Their tears mingled: tears of joy, at being restored and reunited. Then he gently let her back down to her feet. He kissed her deeply and she responded, love overflowing in her heart. He raised his head and smiled at her, his eyes so full of love and devotion.

"Elizabeth, I want you to be my wife, in every true sense of the word: the wife of my heart; the love of my life. And not just because of Mary and Abigail, but because I need you to help me get back to God. I lost my way for a moment, but now I want to find my way back, and I need you to help me. Will you do that for me?"

"Yes, William," Elizabeth laughed happily, holding her husband close. "Yes, yes, yes."

He smiled in contentment. Free at last, happy and fulfilled, he took her hand and led her to the door.

"I never welcomed you properly. Mrs. Edwards, step over the threshold, and welcome home."

The End

A MAIL ORDER MARRIAGE MISTAKE

PROLOGUE

Emma Thomas shivered in her four poster bed. It was the haunting time before dawn where the steady ticking of the hallway clock sounded like hammers in the air. Though Emma was curled up tightly beneath layers of bedding, the seventeen-year-old still felt cold. Lately she has been having sensations of being watched. It was foolish, a product of her fears of the future and marriage, her mother assured her, but alone in her bed with only the sound of the clock and the thumping of her heart, Emma was afraid.

Eyes shut, she prayed, 'Dear Lord,' and the words of Psalm 56, verses 3-4 came up through her mind, 'When I am afraid, I put my trust in you. In God, whose word I praise, in God I trust; I shall not be afraid. What can flesh do to me?'

'What could it?' Emma reassured herself.

Yes, she would be brave. Emma opened her eyes and sat up, pushing the bedding aside and walking to the window. Defiantly, she opened her bedroom curtains and then sat again on the bed, looking around the room that was her sanctuary in her parents' house.

The walls of Emma's room were soft pink as were her curtains. The large princess four poster bed took up almost a quarter of the room, right opposite the large windows that took up the whole of one wall. In summer she had to use sheers to keep out the overly bright sunlight, but in spring the light was moderate and she would then spend hours and hours seated at her vanity table writing poetry and reading.

Much as Emma loved her bedroom and bed she sometimes felt that her mother had gone a little overboard with it. There were pink frills all over the bed and once in a while Emma wished she could rip them all off and leave the bed plain. To worsen matters, her vanity table and stool were also pink. She loved pink but felt that too much of it was more of a bother than beautiful. However, she chose to suffer in silence, humoring her mother whose every waking moment was wrapped up in her husband or her only child. Emma understood when her father locked himself in his study for long hours to escape his wife's ministrations, which he sometimes grumbled to Emma were smothering him.

Enough woolgathering. It was too early to ask to be dressed in her day gown, but she couldn't sit in here any longer either, alone with the clock and the lingering phantoms of her night time fears.

Emma wrapped herself in her dressing gown and made for the large kitchen at the back of the house where she knew Elizabeth would be in the process of preparing breakfast. Her parents were still asleep; they had been out attending the wedding of one of her father's associates' daughters. Though it was early, Bess would give Emma a glass of steaming hot tea with milk and tell her stories that would soon have her laughing, all fear forgotten.

"There is my little lamb," Elizabeth Statton announced, a big smile on her plump face. "Come to sneak some bread and honey in before breakfast?"

"Oh, Bess," Emma almost ran into the arms of her nanny, the woman who had been with the Thomas family even before she was born.

"What is wrong, lambkin?" Bess held out her arms and Emma took refuge in the arms that had held her many nights and the hands that had wiped away her tears and bandaged her bruises over the years. "You seem frightened."

"I felt it again, Bess, as though someone was watching me, and a cold hand was squeezing my heart," the young girl shivered. "I'm scared."

"Come and sit down little one." Bess led the frightened girl to the large round kitchen table. Usually this room cheered Emma up because of the warmth from the large modern coal stove that her father had bought a few months ago, as well as the delicious aroma of baking. Elizabeth had tried to teach Emma how to bake and even though the lessons had been mostly filled with laughter, Emma was a keen learner and could bake simple cakes and pies. Her mother frowned upon her visits to the kitchen, believing that her only daughter should not dirty her hands but leave all the chores for the servants, of whom the Thomas household had plenty.

But this morning, none of that held her interest. Her fear lingered, and as she sat down she refused to let go of Bess's hand.

"Remember what I always tell you, lambkin, you never have to be afraid for God is always watching you," Bess said, and Emma nodded. "Remember the cross that your mama gave you for your fifteenth birthday?"

Instinctively, Emma's free hand went to her neck and she touched the gold cross. She had never taken it off from the moment her mother had put it around her neck. The cross and chain were made of pure gold, and the craftsman had made the chain so strong that it could not easily break.

"Lambkin, that cross is not a talisman, but it represents life for all mankind. As long as you look to the cross for answers you will always be alright and all will be well."

But later that morning when Emma had gone to call on another of her young friends and Bess was setting up the tea tray for the afternoon, she was troubled.

Emma was a sensitive girl, yes, but not prone to vapors. Even as a child she had been fearless, never backing down from any challenge. She had learned how to walk when she was only nine months old and kept moving from that moment onwards. She was the darling of the household and all the servants loved the petite girl with her blond hair and hazel eyes, and even now, as a seventeen-year-old who had turned into a true beauty, she was still loved deeply by the servants.

From the moment Emma was born and her socialite mother Clarissa Thomas had placed the little babe in Bess's arms, the woman had felt such deep love for the child. She was appointed as Emma's wet nurse because her own son Trevor who was six months was already showing signs of stopping his nursing. Being Emma's wet nurse had created a deep bond between Emma and Elizabeth and the two were very close.

Bess shook her head. For the last few weeks, her charge had showed signs of being very scared and the older woman did not take it lightly. She would be very cautious and keep a watchful eye on all the happenings in and around the house. She only wished Trevor were home from the high seas. The boy would know what to do...

Thanks for Reading!

I hope you enjoyed this sample.

If you want to read more of this book, look for the next book in the collection: A Mail Order Marriage Mistake!

All the best, Montana

ABOUT THE AUTHOR

Ever since she was a child watching Westerns like Hondo and the Big Valley with her dad, Montana West has always had a fascination with the Wild West. Now she lives on her Indiana farm with her husband, Jim, two cats, four horses and an elderly goat named Bluebeard. Montana and Jim are avid collectors of the work of artists of the American West, her favorites of the Hudson River School whose artists like Thomas Hill celebrated nature through their transformative works.

Montana hopes that her readers enjoy her work as much as she has enjoyed the great works of other writers and artists fascinated with the American West.

Made in United States
Troutdale, OR
06/06/2025